This book is due

DATE DUE

10-4-16		
12-8-16		
1-11-17		

This book is dedicated to the

2012-2013 Phoenix Five:

Sheridan Spencer,

Andrew Duffy,

Lily Bader-Huffman,

Vanessa Riley,

and Jagger.

Forgive me.

LICENSE TO SPILL

A PRETENDERS NOVEL

BY #1 *NEW YORK TIMES* BESTSELLING AUTHOR

LISI HARRISON

SCHOLASTIC INC.

ISBN 978-0-545-90660-9

Copyright © 2014 by Lisi Harrison. All rights reserved.
Published by Scholastic Inc., 557 Broadway, New York, NY 10012,
by arrangement with Little, Brown Books for Young Readers, a division of
Hachette Book Group, Inc. SCHOLASTIC and associated logos are trademarks
and/or registered trademarks of Scholastic Inc.

12 11 10 9 8 7 6 5 4 3 2 1   15 16 17 18 19 20/0

Printed in the U.S.A.   40

This edition first printing, September 2015

LICENSE TO SPILL

October 2012

I know X-actly what you're thinking. I read your comments online; I hear you whispering in the halls. Many of you say it straight to my face because you don't know I'm X. Things like: "*Pretenders* had zero resolution." "You call that an ending?!" "Will Duffy win his friends back? Does Lily get pulled from Noble High? Arrested for stalking? Both? Who is sending threats to Vanessa? Can Sheridan stop Octavia from stealing the show? And who is Jagger? Simply put, that was 292 pages of cliff-hanger, 0 pages of closure."

Don't worry, *License to Spill* will be much more satisfying. I ended *Pretenders* abruptly to see if you wanted more. And it seems like you do. Which means this is no longer *my* crime, it's *ours*: the Phoenix Five's for keeping secrets, me for spilling them, and yours for soaking them up. Remove any one of these players and no one gets hurt. It takes all three.

Which role did you play?

Not that I care. I'm just glad you came back for more.

Jagger

Oct. 12.

Dad just left my bedroom but not before a thorough interrogation.

> Q: Son, are you aware of the time?
> (10:16 PM.)
> A: No.

> Q: You missed curfew.
> A: My bike chain fell off.

> Q: Why didn't you call?
> A: Battery died.

Q: You said you were getting a ride to Octavia's party.

A: My friend got food poisoning. Anyway, biking is better for the environment.

Dad said, good point. He likes when I think on a global scale.

I yawned and told him I needed sleep. What I really needed was for him to cut the third degree because my forehead was starting to sweat. It must be the secrets inside of me trying to get out. I'm leaking lies. My skin can't hold them back. If they get out

I'd.

Be.

Ruined.

Audri would know the real me. My parents would know the fake me. And I'd go back to being the old me.

Only worse.

Way worse.

Like if Way Worse got jumped by Total Disaster, Living Nightmare, and Public Humiliation and the whole thing was posted on YouTube. Translated into 130 languages. Turned into a cautionary tale and sold in a boxed set with *The Boy Who Cried Wolf* and *The Fall of Icarus*.

Like that.

Only worse.

Way, way worse.

-J

Sheridan

INT. BEDROOM—NIGHT.

SHERIDAN SPENCER taps "play" on her iPhone. Pink's "F**kin' Perfect" begins.

My night was a F**kin' Disaster.

It started when I asked Lily Bader-Huffman if she thought Duffy invited her to the fashion show as his date. I was merely trying to assess the motivation behind her glossy hair and tight red dress. She started crying and then bolted. Now I feel all Guilty Hawn.

Shortly thereafter I accepted Octavia's last-minute party invite when I should have known it was a trap. She wasn't looking for a fresh start. She wanted to prove that Logan was using me for Dad's BMW M3 GTR. And she did, super publicly, thankyouverymuch.

I was so humiliated my limbs seized up. So when Duffy called and Logan answered and told Duffy that he was my boyfriend I was powerless to stop him. I just tried to call Duffy, but he sent me straight to voice mail so that's all messed up too.

But the worst part of my night is the result of a different terrible night. One that haunts me like Banquo's ghost haunts Macbeth in "The Scottish Play" whose title I shall never mention because every actor knows it's bad luck to do so. Only instead of Banquo, this harbinger of regret comes in the way of Vanessa Riley, that smart girl from my science class. The one who saw me torch my Massie Block scarf with a Bunsen burner. The one who somehow knows about that joyride I took with Logan.

It turns out the salesman who got blamed for taking the car was her brother, A.J. Now I have 72 hours to make Dad rehire him at the dealership or Vanessa is going to rat me out. Feeling dizzy.

I need soda.

No, a snack.

No, a rainbow.

Skittles.

CUT.

To Be Continued...

END SCENE.

Duffy

Friday

Officer Boyle showed up five minutes after I called 911. I thought he'd come inside and wait for Lily to get home so he could question her about stealing my personal belongings and hiding them in *her* closet. But he just hung on my porch and asked *me* a bunch of questions.

COP: Has she been lurking?

ME: Lurking?

COP: You know, hiding in the bushes? Following you?

ME: No.

COP: Calling you several times a day?

ME: No.

COP: Watching you with surveillance equipment?

ME: How would I know?

COP: True. Sending inappropriate gifts?

ME: No.

COP: Showing up the moment you need saving?

ME: Huh? No. I mean, yes! I Wiped down the stairs once and she helped me up.

COP: How did you react?

ME: I thanked her.

COP: After you thanked her, did she leave or linger?

ME: Linger.

COP: What did you do?

ME: I gave her a dollar.

COP: Why?

ME: I thought she was waiting for a tip.

COP: A tip?

ME: You know, for helping.

He wrote something on his pad. I tried to peek. He tilted it toward his badge.

COP: Has she ever manipulated a situation so she could be alone with you?

Feeling = Yes! Lily was always in my room buying Trendemic clothes. She was my best customer. But my job has to stay a secret so I withheld evidence.

ME: No.

Feeling = Does he know I'm lying?

COP: Have you told your parents about this?

ME: They're out.

He closed his notebook. It sounded like a slap across the face. Felt like one too.

COP: This girl needs guidance.

GUIDANCE? GUIDANCE? GUIDANCE? GUY DUNCE! Lily is a GUY DUNCE!

Officer Boyle started walking down the porch steps.

ME: That's it? *Guidance?*

COP: What do you want from me, kid?

Feeling = Why do police officers say slick things like "kid"?

ME: Arrest her!

COP: For what?

ME: Stealing? Stalking? Being weird!

COP: Weirdness is a tough thing to prove.

ME: My things were in her closet!

COP: Why were *you* in her closet?

Feeling = Whose side is he on?

ME: My dogs led me there.

COP: Incredible creatures, aren't they?

ME: I guess.

COP: Did you take your things back?

ME: No.

COP: Why?

ME: I didn't want to tamper with a crime scene.

Officer Boyle laughed when I said that. Not the way Hud and Coops do when I Wipe. More how Mandy did when I told her Robert Pattinson has chlorine-eyes. Like, wow-interesting-point.

COP: Sounds like an innocent crush to me.

ME: *Innocent?*

COP: You're a good-looking boy, Andrew, and you're at that age. Girls are going to do some wild things to get your attention. Get used to it, son. Heck, enjoy it. There are worse problems, kid.

ME: Can you at least give her that thing Chris Brown got after he punched Rihanna?

COP: A restraining order?

ME: Yeah.

Right when he started writing up the order a call came in on his walkie-talkie. The public bathrooms at Regal Park had been vandalized.

Feeling = He should have said: I'm knee-deep in an investigation. Assign someone else. But he looked at me and said: Duty calls.

Feeling = He said *duty*.

I would have cracked up if Hud and Coops were there. But they weren't. They aren't talking to me. So even though my face wanted to laugh at "duty" my brain wouldn't let it.

He tore the restraining order off his pad and handed it to me. It said:

I.D.E.A.L.

I—Ignore.

DE—Don't Engage.

A—Avoid.

L—Leading her on.

9

ME: Shouldn't it say something about Lily going to jail if she takes my things again?

COP: Speak to your parents, follow my instructions, and you should be fine.

ME: But—

COP: Get used to it, Heartbreaker.

Then he left.

Feeling = Heartbreaker?!

Am I really the kind of guy girls have crushes on? (Not including Lily because I still think she has a mental disorder.) Relatives call me "handsome" and Mandy's friends say things like, "What a little hottie," but I figured they were just trying to make me blush. I started to wonder what Sheridan thought but I made myself stop because the guy we wanted to ship to Vietnam is now answering her phone and that hurts.

Anyway, I was on the porch thinking about all this when I heard skateboard wheels grinding along the pavement.

Lily rolled up my driveway with leaves in her hair and a scrape on her knee. She looked like she'd clawed her way out of a grave which made me wonder what else she's capable of.

Feeling = Stay calm.

Feeling = I couldn't.

I ran inside.

She started throwing rocks at my bedroom window.

Feeling = This is not an innocent crush.

LILY: I can help you, I can help you!

Feeling = The old rescue thing again.

10

Feeling = Officer Boyle needs to hear this.

I was about to record her when Mrs. Bader-Huffman pulled her inside.

Feeling = I am sleeping with Bubbie Libby until Mom and Dad get home.

— LATER

Lily

Saturday, October 13, 2012

I wasn't even close to done with my previous entry when Mom came into my room.

"Shut your journal," she said.

I wrapped up with a quick sentence about lying on Blake's belly searching the sky for shooting stars. I wanted to write about the policeman who busted Blake and me for hanging on the roof of Noble High. How I made Blake go back to Octavia's party to find Vanessa so she'd hack into the computer and change my grades. How Blake said everything he could to cheer me up about my non-date with Duffy, but Mom said, "Now!"

"Would you mind telling me what happened out there tonight?"

"It's a big world, Nora, could you be more specific?"

"Alan!" she called. "Can you come in here?"

I knew I was being rude. I knew Mom didn't deserve it. I didn't care. I wanted to make her angry. I wanted to know that my behavior affected her. That she loved me enough to hate me. Because the opposite of love isn't hate, it's indifference. And I didn't think I'd survive the night if one more person acted like I didn't matter.

"What's going on?" Dad asked safely from the doorway. He's a bloodhound when it comes to sniffing out tension, a scaredy-cat when it comes to dealing with it.

"Bottom line?" Mom said. "Eight years ago I gave up my career as a child psychologist to homeschool our daughter. Then one day she begged me to let her try public school and against my better judgment, I gave in. Now, after six short weeks, everything I taught her, everything she was"—Mom snapped her fingers—"is gone."

"How can you say that?" I asked.

"Let's see." Mom tapped her chin. "You've been coming home late from school, you joined some style club that has you dressing like a European club kid, you lied about your plans tonight, I just found you throwing rocks at the neighbors' windows—"

"No," I said. "How can you say 'six short weeks' when all weeks are seven days? It doesn't make sense."

"Enough!" Dad snapped. (Finally!) "What's going on, Lily?"

I considered the truth: that I'm a sheltered veal trying

to make it in a free-range world. And that I was foolhardy enough to believe that Andrew Duffy, the leader of that free-range world, wanted to be my guide. With his green eyes and careless hair. His basketball skills and Nike gear, his hoodies and video game high scores. His insouciant gait, loud music, spicy energy drinks, popular sister, nameless dogs, seasonal lawn decorations, and friends with monosyllabic nicknames.

Guys like that don't like girls like me. With my diarrhea-brown eyes and frizzy hair. My useless ability to quote the classics and say the alphabet backward in under a minute. My Encyclopaedia Britannicas and frumpy wardrobe. My highlighter manicures, kosher sandwiches, obsession with the word "Coxsackie," my intellectual Homies, and my best friend, Blake, who refuses to tell anyone he's gay.

If Sheridan Spencer didn't tell me that Duffy's invitation to the fashion show wasn't a date, I might still think I had a chance. For that I blame my parents.

Sheltering me from the public school system made me book smart, but socially illiterate. Maybe if Mom taught me how to read *people* instead of Latin I wouldn't have needed Sheridan Spencer to translate Duffy. I wouldn't have had my hair straightened or my makeup done. I wouldn't have worn a dress. A tight one. A red one! I wouldn't have been skateboarding alone in the dark, crying. Tears wouldn't have blurred my vision and I wouldn't have fallen. I wouldn't have scraped my knee or landed in a pile of leaves.

A police car was backing out of Duffy's driveway as I

rounded the corner, and I couldn't help wondering if maybe Blake had been right. What if something was wrong with Duffy? Something serious? What if he had every intention of meeting me but couldn't? Like in *An Affair to Remember* when Terry is supposed to meet Nickie on the observation deck of the Empire State Building and is hit by a car. Nickie eventually gives up, never knowing that she is in the hospital....

I rolled up Duffy's driveway all worried. He was standing on his porch. I smiled with relief and hurried toward him to make sure he was okay, but he ran inside and slammed the door.

I stood there for a moment, dumbfounded. Did he really just do that? Because pretending someone doesn't exist when they're standing two feet away is a bold move. So bold that it had me thinking I was a ghost. Like my figurative feelings of invisibility had turned me invisible for real.

Since I hadn't done a single thing to elicit this kind of reaction, I suspected something sinister was at play. Like maybe he was being held hostage. And somehow he notified the police but his captor caught on and forced him to get rid of the Boys in Blue. After which he was told to run back inside or the whole family would be blown to bits, starting with the nameless dogs....

As I was contemplating my next move, an upstairs light flicked on, then off. He was trying to communicate. I threw a rock to let him know I was here for him.

When he didn't respond, I called, "I can help you! I can help you! I will!"

That's when Mom pulled me inside and sent me to my room, which smells a lot like dog poo for some reason. Maybe because everything in my life has turned to—

"Lily, answer your father," Mom pressed. "What is going on with you? We're starting to worry."

I couldn't go into the whole thing so I said, "My plans got all messed up, that's all. I was expecting Van Gogh's *The Starry Night* and it turned into Munch's *The Scream*. You've always taught me to manage my expectations and you were right. Lesson learned."

Mom smiled proudly. Then I did too. She still isn't sure what's gotten into me lately and I still don't have a clue why Duffy is ignoring me. But that moment proved that we both matter. And that's all we really wanted to know.

Lily Bader-Huffman-Duffy

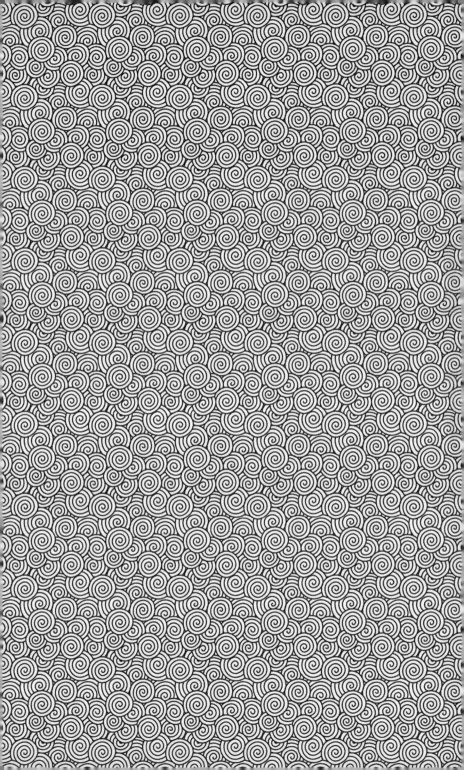

Jagger

Oct. 13.

So there I am, putting marmalade on my toast, when out of nowhere Mother drops the F-bomb.

— A *facial*, I say. Why would *I* want a *facial*?

— I can see the congestion in your pores from across the table. And that's without my readers.

I say it's probably a rash or something. But I know it's not. It's my lies. They're trying to get out.

As soon as she leaves for tennis I put on my ski pants, a thermal, my Vampire Weekend tee, a wool sweater, and a hat.

I set the timer in the sauna for twenty minutes and get in.

After one minute I find it hard to breathe.

After three minutes my vision blurs.

After five I slump over.

My cheek lands on the metal hook of my old ski pass. It burns. I scream. I stumble toward the door handle.

I step into the bathroom and guzzle the cool air.

I yank off my clothes.

My chest is purple. My left cheek has been branded with two red lines.

I lean closer to the mirror to see if five minutes was enough to sweat out my lies.

I'm so dizzy I fall down.

Ms. Silver comes to me in a dream.

She says journals are a safe place for unpopular thoughts and tells me to bury my lies in these pages.

I ask if that will free up my pores.

She says my pores and my brain.

I say, okay.

Anything to keep Mother from dropping another F-bomb.

LIE #1: My parents, Carla and Ed, were sent to jail on February 13, 2011 for bully beating.

LIE #2: They are on death row.

LIE #3: A social worker came and took me away the day they were arrested.

LIE #4: I've been emancipated since I was fourteen.

LIE #5: I live in the back room of Randy's Exotic Pets.

LIE #6: Randy lets me live there as long as I feed his pets at night.

LIE #7: Randy meets with international pet dealers who carry guns.

LIE #8: I hop the train to Manhattan to visit my parents in jail. (Is there even a jail in Manhattan? I should probably find out.)

LIE #9: Mom is a health teacher. Dad is a pharmacist.

LIE #10: I can sign my own permission slips and report cards.

LIE #11: I stole a bike.

LIE #12: I am being followed by an ex–navy SEAL named Crazy Pat who is seeking revenge for Pat Jr., the bully my parents beat.

LIE #13: I told Audri that FemFresh pen came inside my journal bag.

LIE #14: I said I thought FemFresh was an organic food company.

LIE #15: I won a debate on the death penalty because my parents are on death row.

LIE #16: I told Audri I know what it feels like to lose a family. I said I cry about it.

LIE #17: I told Audri that Crazy Pat was at Octavia's party.

LIE #18: Everything I told Father last night was a lie. (Even my yawn. I wasn't tired at all.)

(LIE #19: My first initial is J.)

Vanessa

October 13th

I just paused *SNL* right in the middle of Christina Applegate's opening monologue so I could journal. Because when I write I can't scratch. If I can't scratch, my arms won't look like they've been beaten by Twizzlers.

Ver? I miss middle school. Life was so rewarding[62] back then. I was a role model, model citizen, and lead model in the Fashion for Felines fund-raiser at the pet rescue center. Now everything is so complicated and so so itchy. Everyone said Noble High would be hard but I didn't think it would be hard for *me*. Just average people. Oh my god, what if I'm average?

....

[62] Literally. I have 159 awards.

ITCHY!

I know I shouldn't think about it, but I can't stop. I shouldn't have left Lily on the roof of Noble last night. I should have hacked her grades like I promised. So what if she stole Blake from me. If I hacked her grades instead of holding a grudge, she wouldn't be able to tell on me for hacking my own because she'd be guilty too.

Now she's sending snail-mail threats. Here's the latest:

I KNEW YOU WERE UP TO SOMETHING.
NOW I HAVE PROOF.

Ahhhhhhhhhhhhhhhhhhhh! So itchy so so so itchy so so sooooooooo . . . I have to scratch. . . .

UGH!

To live in uncertainty is to die scratching.[63]

At least I found a way to get A.J. his job back at the BMW dealership. Correction, I confronted the girl who stole the car and let my brother take the blame. Turns out it was Sheridan Spencer, the boss's daughter. I told that unethical Barbie she better make things right or I'd take her down.

. . . Unless Lily takes me down first.

I can't let her. She can't take Blake and my pride in the same month. I won't let her. I'd sooner turn myself in.[64]

---

[63] Doesn't that sound profound?

[64] I bet there's a prize for being honest; like a Medal of Martyrdom or a Ribbon of Reform.

Hmmm...

I could blame my lapse in judgment on my unstable home life. Principal Alden would feel sorry for me and let me off with a warning. News of my hacking would go viral and soon I'd be fielding job offers from Microsoft and Apple. Of course I'd turn them down...at least until I was sure Mom and Dad's marriage was back on track. Which of course it would be the moment they realized that their constant fighting drove me to hack in the first place.

O my G. Problem solved. Forgive me, Principal Alden, for I have sinned....

Now back to Christina.

DUFFY

Monday

I am sitting on a bench outside Abercrombie & Fitch waiting for Mandy to pick up her paycheck. I think she picked up an extra shift too because she's been in there for twenty-five minutes.

A little girl just threw a handful of pennies in the water fountain and didn't make a wish.

Feeling = What a waste.

If I had a handful of pennies I'd ask the fountain to make my life stop sucking.

I just checked my backpack for change. I don't have a single coin.

Feeling = Even my backpack is in the red.

Anyway, things are so bad I need more than a few wishes. I need a miracle. All because the guys on the team saw me running on King's Lane Friday night. Running, when I was supposed to be home with a sore leg. I hoped everything would blow over by today but it just blew harder. The entire practice was one big joke. And I was the punch line.

Why did Duffy spend all day in the bathroom? HE HAS THE RUNS.

Who is Duffy's favorite rapper? RUN-D.M.C.

What's Duffy's favorite country? I-RAN.

It was getting so bad I wanted to tell Hud and Coops the truth about the Trendemic fashion show. But I couldn't. They'd ask why I had to go to a fashion show in the first place and I'd have to tell them about the money I owe Anton which would make me have to tell them about Dad being in the red and Dad made me promise not to tell anyone, especially Hud because his father's real estate company is the competition. So I had to take it.

My only shot at winning them back was to go off during the scrimmage and make them realize that even if they didn't like me, they needed me.

So when Coach Bammer blew his whistle I charged the ball like the Pamplona bull that chased Bubbie Libby and Grandpa Stu through Spain on their honeymoon.

I scored when Ryan elbowed me in the rib.

I scored when Steve rubbed his pit sweat on my cheek.

I scored when Logan sneezed, "RUN, old McDonald."

Then I scored eight more times. Did they stop busting on me? No. They cracked jokes during stretches and showers too. But no one said they wanted me off the team.

Feeling = It worked.

Then Coach stopped me on my way out.

COACH BAMMER: Duffy?

ME: Yeah.

COACH BAMMER: Great playing today.

ME: Thanks.

COACH BAMMER: Better than great. Miraculous.

ME: Aw, cool.

COACH BAMMER: What did you eat today?

ME: Huh?

COACH BAMMER: Must be some new Super Food on the market.

I thought he was joking so I tried to laugh.

COACH BAMMER: No, for real. In twenty-seven years of coaching I've never seen an ankle heal so fast.

Feeling = Uh-oh.

If Coops was there he would have said, "Ankle heal? Make up your mind, Coach. Is it the ankle or the heel?" But he was long gone.

COACH BAMMER: So tell me, how did you do it?

ME: Ice, heat, ice, heat . . . you know.

COACH BAMMER: With all that heat you'll be great at your new position on the Flames.

ME: New position?

COACH BAMMER: Congratulations, Mr. Duffy. You're our new bench warmer.

Feeling = No. Please, please, please, no. I can't sit. I have to play. You can't do this to me. Please don't do this to me!

ME: But—

COACH BAMMER: This is a team sport and you abandoned your team by faking an injury.

ME: But we're playing the Meadowlarks on Friday. You *need* me.

COACH BAMMER: I need dedication and reliability, that's what I need.

ME: I am those things, I swear! Let me play, Coach, please! It won't happen again, I promise.

COACH BAMMER: You're suspended, Duffy. I expect to see you on that bench, on time, for every game and practice or you're off Varsity.

ME: For how long?

COACH BAMMER: Until that cold bench is good and warm.

Feeling = I'm done.

Then right when I was leaving the gym something cool happened—

TIME OUT! I just saw Blake go into J.Crew. That means Lily could be around. Going to hide.

— LATER

Sheridan

10.15.12

INT. THE HONEY BUN—LATE AFTERNOON.

SHERIDAN sits solo at a table for two as pedestrians scuttle past the bakery's rain-streaked window. She makes peace with the weather and the fact that she's sitting alone in public. Her extra-large Peanut Butter Frozen Hot Chocolate with Whip is too sweet for salty thoughts.

One could argue that drinking this extra-large peanut butter frozen hot chocolate with whip is pointless because I am already full of delight. But it's more of a celebration libation than a mindless indulgence. Because yes, Virginia, I had a glorious day.

I channeled Drew Barrymore because I needed a serious take two on my social status and she's had more comebacks than a boomerang. My biggest challenge was committing to a look. Drew does hippie, rocker, glam, pregnant, and frump equally well. Then I began to wonder why Drew has had so many successful comebacks. Rather, why her and not Britney or Lindsay?

It came to me after a sip of whip and a moment of brain freeze. Drew is free, easy, and open to change. She doesn't dwell on the dark days of yesteryear. She lives for the sunny possibilities of tomorrow. That's how I want to be. So I chose hippie Drew.

Hair: air-dried in twists for a beachy wave; one braid, left side.

Costume: loose white tee, worn denim jacket, ruffled brown skirt (long), wood accessories.

Makeup: mascara, dash of cheek glitter, cherry ChapStick.

Attitude: glow, flow, put on a show.

Objectives: threefold.

1. Make Dad rehire Vanessa's brother, A.J.
2. Coexist with Octavia since I can't afford to ship her *and* Logan to Vietnam.
3. Convince Duffy that Logan is not my boyfriend.

My opportunity came after *Wicked* rehearsals.

FLASHBACK. INT. SCHOOL HALLWAY OUTSIDE THE THEATER—LATE AFTERNOON.

SHERIDAN waits outside the bathroom for AUDRI so they can walk home together.

You're not still bummed are you? (Octavia.)

About what? (Me. Seriously wondering where this is going.)

The whole Logan thing.

What "Logan thing"? (Me, making air quotes.)

Octavia raised her blond brows the way Mom does when I make unhealthy food choices. Like, *Really? You're gonna go there?*

He pretended to like you so he could drive your dad's car but he really likes me. (Octavia, all smuggy.) *I'd be bummed if someone used me like that so I was just checking to make sure you're okay.*

Drew's spirit whispered in my ear. *Fake her out, Sheridan. Set her up. Play off her ego. Do it!*

Even though I knew Logan used me, I took Drew's advice and switched the script.

You think Logan used me for my dad's car? (Me, acting.)

Octavia fake-pouted. *I do. I'm so sorry.*

I put my hand on her bony shoulder and fake-pouted back. *Actually, he was using you so the Flames would have a place to party after the game.* (Thank you, improv lessons.)

High-lare! (Octavia.) *You seriously believe that?*

Yes (no), *and I can prove it.*

How?

Ask Logan if he wants to take another ride in the M3 GTR and watch him say no. (Me, setting her up.)

What'll that prove?

That he went on that ride to be with me, not the car.

What if he says yes? (Octavia.)

Then I'll give you the keys.

And if he says no?

Then you have to admit he likes me for me and let me have him back. (This won't happen so I'm not worried.)

Deal. Octavia offered me her right hand. We shook. Her rings dug into my skin.

Then the gym doors popped open and the Flames came out, all wet-haired and soap-scented.

It's show time. (Me, encouraging her.)

Sheridan, tell Owdee I had to run. (Octavia.)

Will do. (Will won't.)

When I realized I might see Duffy, I ran in the bathroom like I needed to tell Audri something important.

Digestive tract issues much? (Me, busting on her because she'd been in there for a fortnight.)

Sorry. Have you been waiting for me this whole time? She was standing in front of the mirror, poking a mascara wand down the top of her signature blue-framed glasses.

It's okay, I said, even though it wasn't. Not that I wanted to find Audri all doubled over in a stall clutching her cramping stomach. I didn't. I'd only wish that on Octavia. But these days jazzy eyes meant she was leaving school with someone whose name rhymes with Bragger.

I was right. Jagger (allegedly) "just" texted Audri to remind her of their (alleged) "post-rehearsal plan." A plan she had (allegedly) "forgotten all about."

I was about to question Audri's honesty when Drew told me to let it slide. She did tell me to text Vanessa and ask for an extension until Friday. Extension granted. Drew isn't a Barrymore—she's the Barry*most*!

END FLASHBACK.

CUT TO INT. SCHOOL HALLWAY—FIVE MINUTES LATER.

SHERIDAN leans against a locker and searches her music library for a song to score her friendless journey home. "Maybe" from *Annie*? "What I Did for Love" from *A Chorus Line*? "Lean on Me" from *Glee* season one? Yes, that's the one. She takes a moment to untangle her earbuds. The unexpected pop of the gym door startles her. She looks up. It's DUFFY.

Hey. (Me.)

Hey. (Duffy.)

I'm not stalking you, I swear. (Me, trying to lighten the mood.)

What's that supposed to mean?

You don't know what stalking means?

I know what it means. I'm wondering why you said it.

I looked around the empty hall before I answered. *Um, maybe because I just so happened to be standing here when you came out of the gym. Like. A. Stalker. Would.*

That's it? (Duffy, looking kind of freaked out.) *No other reason?*

No.

So you weren't making a stalking joke on purpose?

34

No! Cheeses, do you seriously think I was stalking you?

He shrugged like it was possible.

Don't flatter yourself, Bieber. (I jammed my earbuds in my ears. I didn't care that the wire was still tangled.) *I was just leaving.*

He didn't try to stop me so I had to keep walking. I hate when that happens.

Better hurry. Your boyfriend left a while ago. (Duffy.)

Ground or Next Day Air? (Me.)

CUT TO EXT. STROLLING—LATE AFTERNOON.

SHERIDAN and DUFFY promenade toward town; lost in conversation, oblivious to the spitting rain.

Now do you believe Logan isn't my boyfriend? (Me.)

Yep. And do you believe I didn't ditch you at the fashion show? (Duffy.)

Believe.

And that I wasn't trying to lead Lily on?

Believe.

And that I don't think I'm Justin Bieber?

Belieb.

Duffy laughed but his eyes still looked sad.

Bad midterm? (Me.)

Lowest grade was a B. (Duffy.)

Same. In what?

Dramatic Arts. You?

Phys Ed. (Me.)

We marveled at the odds of his best subject being my worst and vice versa. Still, his green eyes seemed blue.

What's wrong, then? Did something happen during practice? (Me.)

Kind of, yeah.

We crossed the street without saying a word. Awk-word. (Ha.)

Well, aren't you going to tell me? (Me.)

It's not a big deal. (Duffy.)

Silence again.

You know what is a big deal? (Me.) *Frozen hot chocolate at the Honey Bun. Ever had it?*

Duffy nodded his head, yes. The shaking must have flipped a switch in his brain because the lights came back on behind his eyes. *They have this peanut butter one that—*

Please, I invented it. (Me.) *I get extra large but they only charge me for a large.*

That's so cool.

I know. I save a whole dollar.

No, I mean it's cool that you get those. (Duffy.)

Why?

My sister Mandy would never. She's obsessed with food and weight and stuff. Same with her friends. It's annoying.

My mom is like that. She's always saying things like, "I guess I could have a lick of that lollipop. I ran seventy-five miles today. I deserve it." I swear, it's like, obsess over something that matters. (Me.)

Yeah, like extra whip! (Duffy.)

We laughed.

Seriously, though. I think it's cool that you're just...you know...real.

My heart thumped "That's the sweetest thing ever" in Morse code.

Just as Duffy opened the door to the Honey Bun his skitty (skinny/pretty) sister Mandy pulled up in her car.

Get in! (Mandy.)

Why? (Duffy.)

It's raining. (Mandy.)

So? (Duffy.)

There's a huge storm coming. (Mandy.)

No there isn't. (Duffy.)

You have a dentist appointment.

I do not.

Mom wants to see you right away. (Mandy.)

Why? (Duffy.)

Didn't say. (Mandy.)

Tell her I'll be home soon. (Duffy.)

Better come now. She's pissed. (Mandy.)

Why? Did she see your midterm? (Duffy.)

Unfunny. (Mandy.)

It's okay. (Me, being laid back and cool.) *Go.*

Want a ride? (Duffy.)

No thanks. (Me.)

The rain started to pick up. We just stood there like it was 72 and sunny.

You're going to get a frozen hot chocolate, aren't you? (Duffy.)

Kind of.

No fair. (Duffy.)

Mandy honked the horn. *Let's go!*

Duffy got in the car and pointed a finger gun at his temple. One minute later he sent this text: *Mandy lied. She's dragging me to the mall to get her paycheck. Should have known. She hates driving alone. You owe me a frozen.—Later.*

And that was my day. Pretty sweet, huh? I accomplished my social goals without any help from Audri. Which makes me wonder if I rely on her too much. Because there's a big difference between missing Audri and needing Audri. As big as the difference between the large frozen hot chocolate and the extra-large. Which is big. (Burp.) Trust me.

To Be Continued...

END SCENE.

Vanessa

October 15th

Today Lily was a snail, and I was her trail.

I followed her to every class. I watched her and Blake eat lunch.[65] I pretended to drink from the water fountain while she used the bathroom—once before second period and again after fifth. I wasn't quite ready to turn myself in to Principal Alden, but if Lily was going to rat me out, I wanted to beat her to it.

While forging my final snail trail of the day[66] the unexpected

---

[65] She threw her salami sandwich in the trash. I thought of the Haitian orphans who make my SWAPs. What they wouldn't have done for a bite.

[66] Following Lily to Algebra.

happened. Blake pulled up beside me and pinched my white oxford shirt.

"Someone's looking very Annie Hall today," he said.

I didn't know what Annie Hall meant. Was it an insult or a compliment? Was it a reference to the crowded hall we were in? Luckily, I was still mad at him for ditching me at Octavia's party so I didn't feel the need to say anything at all.

"I'm sorry about Friday night," he said. "Lily called me crying and—"

"And she *is* your girlfriend, so . . ."

"*Girlfriend*?" Blake said, as if I had just accused him of dating a lamp. "Lily's not my girlfriend."

I stopped walking and turned to face him. He needed to see the flecks of seriousness in my green eyes. "That's not what Caprice told me."

His face scrunched up, like I had just burped in his face. "And you believed her?"

I shrugged.

"Vanessa"—his hot fudge–colored eyes warmed—"why would I ask you to go to a party if I had a girlfriend?"

I liked where he was going and immediately wanted more. I wanted him to convince me that Lily was just a friend and I was more. Then I lost my visual on Lily and my arms started to itch.

It was a setup! Blake distracted me so Lily could tell Principal Alden what I had done. How could I be so stupid?

"I have to go!"

"Wait!" Blake called.

I didn't answer. My ears were ringing and my skin was crawling. I ignored the bell and ran straight to Principal Alden's office. His door was closed.

FOE NO YOU DIZN'T!

"Is he in there with someone?" I asked his assistant, Ms. Nadler.

"Principal Alden is meeting with the board members. He'll be back tomorrow. Is it important?"

I sighed so hard the papers on her desk blew. "Did anyone else come to see him? Like in the last minute or so? A girl named Lily?"

Ms. Nadler looked at me over the top of her glasses. "Yes, and I told her the same thing I'm going to tell you. Get. To. Class."

So that's it. Tomorrow, at first light, I turn myself in. I wonder if they have awards in juvie?[67]

> *Surrender to life itself and you'll just be rewarded*
> *with so many things.*
>
> —Jason Mraz

---

[67] The colloquial term for a juvenile detention center. Aka jail.

Lily

Monday, October 15, 2012

Oh, Karess... My buff personal trainer slash DJ on Sundays
who spells C-words with K's... Once upon a time you were
nothing more than a fake journal entry. A device designed to tip
me off if Mom was snooping. But now? By Kupid, I wish you
were real. The idea of Greyhounding it to Florida and opening
a gym together kould not be more appealing right now.

I believe honesty is important in a relationship, in which
case you should know that Andrew Duffy was my first krush,
not you. I still have trace amounts of feelings for him but he has
no interest in me; so no threat there.

I know, I found it hard to believe at first too. How he could go from liking me, even as a friend, to shutting me out with such certitude. I assumed he was being held kaptive in his home, because what other explanation kould there be? Well, Karess, I was wrong. Duffy was at school today and didn't seem the least bit post-traumatic. Meaning, he was really just ignoring me. The worst part is I have no klue why. Every time I got klose enough to ask, he took off. He even turned Bubbie Libby against me.

I arrived to walk their nameless dogs and instead of the usual hair-spray-scented hug, Bubbie Libby relieved me of my duties. She said a girl like me must have better things to do after school and that she was doing me a favor by kutting me loose. I assured her that I liked the job and needed the money but she said, "Kanines aren't kosher. Why should you kompromise your dietary beliefs for an old bubbie like me?"

I said I didn't want to eat them, just walk them. But she held firm and klosed the door in my face.

Trust me, Karess. It gets worse. Mom and Dad are in their bedroom right now whispering about my midterm report kard. Soon they will be standing over my bed, telling me I kan't go to Noble High anymore.

So I'm all yours, Karess. Kome get me anytime.

Until then,

Lily Bader-Huffman.

All I wanted was a chance to live in the real world, but no! It's back to the veal world for me. Mom insisted on straight A's and I got a B+ in Spanish and an A- in Global Media. So I'm done.

Even though I'm mad at Vanessa because she could have saved me by changing my grades, I spent all day wanting to know if "the solution" worked for her. Did she pull it off? Was she paranoid? Would she do it again? But Vanessa didn't want anything to do with me. She made that clear by staying ten feet behind me all day.

Blake said I should confront her, but I didn't have it in me. I'm a loser, not a stalker.

"Will you talk to her?" I asked Blake.

"Why me?"

"It's your fault she hates me. If you hadn't left her at Octavia's party—"

"Lily, you called me collect. You were crying. I didn't leave to leave; I left to see if you were okay. I was being a good friend. And you know what you're being?"

"What?"

"A Coxsackie."

"Why am I the Coxsackie?"

"Because you're acting like this is my fault."

"It *is* your fault!" I snapped. "If you would just come out of the closet and tell Vanessa you're..." I couldn't shout "gay" in the hall or Blake would have had an asthma attack, so I widened my eyes where the word "gay" would go.

"What would that do?"

"She would stop crushing on you and we could all be friends again."

Blake thought about it for a minute. Then he said, "Can't do it."

"Well, what can you do?" I snapped. "Because right now you're my only friend and I'm about to have a very needy year. So unless you're prepared to be on call for me twenty-four/seven I suggest you fix this."

Blake took a puff on his inhaler and then handed me his New York Giants zipper binder. "Hold this, I'll be right back." And off he went.

I had a few minutes before Algebra so I hurried to Principal Alden's to see if there was anything I could do to boost my grades, but Ms. Nadler said he was gone until tomorrow. I told her that tomorrow was too late. I needed to speak with the principal today. She told me to get to class. So I did. With Blake's binder. He was docked 10 percent for not having his English homework so now he's mad at me too.

Mom and Dad just came in.

Standing above me now.

Glaring.

It burns.

Lily

Monday, October 15, 2012

Janis Joplin sang, "Freedom's just another word for nothing left to lose," and if that's true I, Lily Bader-Huffman, am free.

All I wanted was a chance to explore life beyond these walls. To acclimate, infiltrate, participate. To make my mark. Now that I'm a Homie again, the only mark I'll ever make is a giant ?

What would have become of Lily if her parents had let her stay in public school? Would she have won Duffy's heart? Or a swim meet? Or a scholarship? Would she have gotten kicked out of class for laughing? Served detention? Skipped lunch with her new best friends? Would she have tried out for the cheerleading squad? Or run for student council? Or tried bacon? Or missed curfew? Or had a yearbook? Or gotten asked to prom? Or been valedictorian? Or had a first kiss?

No one will ever know. Not only because I, Lily Bader-Huffman, will cease to have typical teen experiences, but also because I am no longer required to write about them in this journal.

Yes, Karess, this means goodbye to you too. Kall me, maybe.

Lily Bader-Huffman-Duffy

Jagger

Oct. 17.

I was giving Audri a ride home when I noticed it.

My bike was harder to pedal today than it had been yesterday or Monday or any of the days last week.

Our backpacks weren't extra full. Our jean jackets were thin. Mine even had holes.

So why the extra weight?

Think, Jagger...think!

It got even harder to pedal as we passed Randy's Exotic Pets.

That's when I knew.

I was pedaling for three.

Me. Audri. And my lies.

Hiding them in this journal cleared my pores, not my conscience.

I have to come clean.

Not because I'm the Warren Buffett of honesty or anything.

More because Audri makes New Jersey smell like vanilla. She isn't afraid to wear blue-framed glasses. She calls making out "baking trout." Her favorite animal is a sugar glider. She drew a tiny J on her tennis skirt for good luck. And when you know little things like that about someone, you want them to know little things like that about you.

Real things.

The kind of things that turn like into love.

Five hours later Audri and I are in the ravine.

It's dark.

The glow-stick crown I made helps her see. It's pink.

Mine is yellow. No way am I wearing pink.

Audri asks why we're creeping through the woods behind some rich person's estate.

I offer her one of the Adirondack chairs I dragged across the lawn after dinner.

She sits.

I sit.

The crescent moon reminds me of her crooked smile.

I ask if she remembers that secret she told me. About seeing her mom bake trout with some guy who isn't her dad.

She says no.

Then she laughs and says of course she does. It's not the kind of thing a person forgets.

Audri's awesome sarcasm gives me a tingle behind my belt.

I say I have a secret to tell her. A big one.

She leans forward. The pink crown slips down her forehead and rests on top of her glasses. She leaves it there. She's *that* all ears.

I say she can't tell anyone.

She crosses her heart, but really, it's where her boobs are.

I feel that behind my belt too.

I begin my confession by asking if she's ever heard of Legacy Hygienics.

She says, of course. Everyone has.

It's true. Legacy Hygienics is the largest manufacturer of hygiene products in North America. They make soap, baby wipes, shampoos, feminine products, lotions, ointments, deodorants, and money.

Lots and lots of money.

They are a family-owned company, I tell her.

Lucky family, she says.

Lucky me, I say back. That family is mine.

Audri gasps.

I explain.

The company was started in 1953 by Morris Ponnowitz—a real family guy.

Audri says, like the cartoon?

I laugh, then say not even close. He was my grandfather.

He knew that people care about their families more than anything. So he made products that families would value from factories that felt like home.

In 1960, Legacy started free after-school programs and summer camps for the kids of employees. They gave away Disney vacations to workers with straight-A students. Soon everyone wanted a job at Legacy, especially his own son.

When the son was eight, Grandfather created Mini Mavericks, a business club for kids who dreamed of working at Legacy one day. Today, that boy is Richard Ponnowitz IV, the CEO. He is also my father. Rosemary Ponnowitz, the girl who sat beside him in the first Mini meeting, is the head of Research and Development. She is my mother.

And I, Daniel Randolph Ponnowitz (not Jagger), am president of that club.

Audri applauds.

I am relieved.

Then I'm not. I haven't gotten to the bad part yet. Now I will.

I ask if she ever had career day.

She did. Sixth grade. Sheridan said if they chose the same career they could share an apartment in New York and eat chocolate croissants three times a day. Audri had always dreamed of living with Sheridan and she loved chocolate croissants so she chose actress.

But deep down inside, Audri wanted to be a street-namer. She lives on Vaji Boulevard and no one pronounces it properly. Instead of Va-hee everyone says Vadg-ee and she wants to change that because it's super embarrassing.

I say I wanted to be president of Legacy Hygienics.

She is not surprised.

I say, you're about to be, and get back to the part about career day.

So I'm in the auditorium. The whole school is there. But I'm not nervous. I'm proud. I have slides, color brochures, and product samples for everyone.

I begin my presentation with the company motto: At Legacy Hygienics we value what you value—Pure Family.

Audri says it sounds great.

I say it was. Until some eighth-grade girl yells YOUR FAMILY MAKES TAMPONS!

(The T-word lands like a punch.)

Audri asks what I did.

I say, I stood there while everyone laughed. Then someone threw a T-word on the stage and they laughed harder.

I should have been born into the Target family instead because that's what I became.

Remember Pat? The guy I said was a navy SEAL? He isn't. He's just a raging bully from my old school.

Pat changed my name from Daniel Ponnowitz to DanPonn. Get it? Sounds like that word I don't like to say.

Audri says it's like her street name.

I smile, but only for a second.

I tell her I spent all three years of middle school being called DanPonn and dodging T-words and wishing I had never been born.

Audri asks if Pat is the guy my parents beat up. If he's the reason they're on death row.

I say no. My parents didn't beat up anyone. They aren't on death row. This is their estate. They are inside right now watching *Jimmy Kimmel Live!*

Audri doesn't say anything. Then she does.

Q: Why the lies?
A: We moved to a new district where no one knew me. I could start over. I could not come from a family that made T-words or have a name that sounds like the word I can't say.

Q: And you thought it was better to come from a family that was going to the electric chair?
A: I know. It's kind of stupid. Pat has a tattoo of an electric chair on his arm. That's how I thought of it, I guess.

Q: Don't you have to be eighteen to get a tattoo?
A: He's in eleventh grade now. His brother is a tattoo artist so . . .

Q: Was he really at Octavia's party?
A: Yeah.

Q: Why?
A: Crashed, I guess.

Q: Why, Jagger?
A: I like it.

Audri says I could have started fresh without making up all those stories.

I say that was the plan. Then one lie led to another and then she happened and I really liked her.

Q: So?
A: So, it isn't me you like. It's Jagger. And I was afraid that you wouldn't like Dan as much.

She says I'm wrong about that.

I say, I am?

She says yeah. I don't like either one of you.

She says she is sick of lies. Her mother lied to her father and that's why they split up.

I promise her the truth from this point on.

Audri says it's too late. She takes off the glow-stick crown and drops it on the Adirondack chair. She says it was nice knowing me...or not knowing me...or whatever that was.

Then she leaves, taking the vanilla smell with her. I feel even heavier than before. So heavy I can't walk to the house. I fall asleep in a bed of leaves and glow-stick crowns and hope I never wake up.

LIE #20: I didn't tell Audri any of that because I don't want her to leave me in the woods. I don't want her to leave me anywhere. Ever.

That's the truth.

Vanessa

October 18th

Great news! I'm not in juvie! Ver? I'm in the kitchen waiting for the Domino's guy[68] thanks to Lily's parents.

According to Blake[69] they made Lily drop out of Noble because she "lost her way." According to my skin, I haven't been this relieved in months.

Those who know and admire me get that I'm not one to find pleasure in the pain of others. And I have dozens of

---

[68] Mom is working late, Dad is still in Las Vegas, and A.J. and I are craving hot wings and cheesy bread.

[69] More on him in a second.

humanitarian awards, including but not limited to a current project with Haitian orphans to prove it. That said, I am also not used to being threatened, so the shedload of jubilation I feel in her absence is totally out of character for me.

Most importantly, Lily has not made any more attempts to contact Principal Alden so I have decided not to confess. Instead, I vow to never, EVER commit said crime again. My focus is back and I'm ready to dominate. At least I will be. Just as soon as things calm down between me and Blake.

Ver? Now that Lily is gone we've put the "in" and "able" in "inseparable" and the "us" in "jealous." I swear, guys whisper when Blake and I walk by. Girls stare in that I-want-to-be-her kind of way. It's like middle school all over again.

Finally!

Duffy

Saturday

Feeling = Like I had been sent to the principal's office. Except it was Saturday and the waiting room didn't smell like ink. Which was a bummer because breathing ink is better than whatever Trendemic was pumping through the vents. I zipped my hoodie over my nose.

The secretary looked like Megan Fox but that's not why I was staring. I was staring because the wall behind her desk was covered in leaves and I swear I saw her pick a few off and eat them.

Feeling = Megan Fox? More like Megan Giraffe.

I put on my headphones and blasted Wiz Khalifa. Then

Sheridan FaceTimed me. I ignored it because I didn't want her to see where I was. I couldn't call her back because she'd hear the Trendemic music and how would I explain gongs and wind chimes? So I texted.

ME: *Hey. What up?*

SHERIDAN: *Where are you? Just FT'ed.*

ME: *Really? Didn't see it. How did it go last night?*

I was talking about the Logan scam. Last I heard Octavia was all pumped up because she asked Logan if he wanted to take the BMW out again and he said yes. Which proves he was using Sheridan for the car, or something like that. I yawned and went deaf when Sheridan explained the setup so I don't completely understand it. Anyway, Logan took the car last night and I couldn't wait for that buttnugget to get caught.

SHERIDAN: *Mission accomplished!*

Feeling = Yes!

SHERIDAN: *Waiting to see if Dad's going to press charges. Fingers crossed.*

ME: *Did A.J. get his job back?*

SHERIDAN: *He will.*

ME: *Yes!*

Then Megan Giraffe asked if I was It Guy #71470.

That's my Trendemic number so I said yeah.

She said, Anton will see you now.

I told Sheridan that I had to walk the dogs, then I followed the Giraffe over a bridge made of video screens. I stepped on some male model's chin with my dirty sneaks.

Feeling = Ha!

Anton was orange as ever. His hair, which was black last Friday, was blond. I thought of that spray-tan mom on You-Tube and laughed inside my mouth.

Giraffe handed Anton a beaker filled with green liquid. He dumped it down the back of his throat and then handed it back to her all smeared and gross. She smiled like he had just given her the new PS3, then bolted.

Feeling = Don't leave me alone with him.

Feeling = Why is he staring at me?

Feeling = Say something!

Feeling = I can't take this anymore.

ME: *What?*

ANTON: You tell me.

ME: Huh?

ANTON: September 24, 2012...

ME:

ANTON: Trendemic lent you two thouuu-zand five hunnn-dred dollars. Of which you have paid back...(He clicked a few buttons on his keyboard)...Four hundred twenty-six.

ME: I know. I'm sorry. I kind of wanted to talk to you about that.

(He was staring again.)

ME: It's not that I don't want to pay you back. I'm trying. It's just been kinda hard.

ANTON: I'm sorry, #71470. How about I DM the Almighty and see if He could make life a little easier for you.

Feeling = Glad my sister Amelia wasn't there. She would have said the Almighty is a She and that would have pissed him off even more.

ME: It's just that you want me to sell glow-in-the-dark skinny jeans and polka-dot turtlenecks and suspenders made of bicycle chains and body spray called Animaul...

ANTON: And?

ME: And the people I know aren't into that stuff.

ANTON: What kind of people are these?

ME: Americans.

He handed me a remote control and clapped twice. The screen behind his desk lit up.

ANTON: You have one more chance. Press the SAVE button every time you see something you can sell. Press NEXT to skip it.

The lights went out and a pair of shorts made from deflated balloons came on the screen.

Feeling = NEXT.

ANTON: It will take three hours to get through all of our products so try not to need me. I'm going to brunch.

ME: But I have basketball practice.

ANTON: Do you have two thousand seventy-four dollars in the pockets of those ill-fitting jeans?

ME: No.

ANTON: Then practice tomorrow.

ME: If I miss this I'll get kicked off the team.

ANTON: Teenage Boy problems.

Feeling = Really, Anton? Because unless you're forcing other dudes to give up basketball so they can shop for Lady Gaga clothes, I'd say this problem is all mine.

—LATER

Sheridan

10.20.12

INT. LIVING ROOM SOFA—LATE AFTERNOON.

SHERIDAN hides behind the plastic potted plant outside her FATHER's study, eavesdropping on the conversation between her DAD, LOGAN, and MR. PRATT (LOGAN's DAD).

Thanks to my well-crafted scheme, Vanessa's brother, A.J., "happened" to be at the dealership when Logan and Octavia returned from *Joyride 2—The Sequel*. According to A.J. this is how it went down.

FLASHBACK.

EXT. SPENCER BMW BACK LOT—NIGHT.

An M3 GTR screeches to a stop. The DRIVER parks

and cuts the engine. The headlights snap off. LOGAN and OCTAVIA emerge from the stolen vehicle, giggling. Believing they've gotten away with their crime, they exchange a victorious high five. OCTAVIA suggests celebrating with Mike's Hard Punch when a dark figure emerges from behind the SERVICE GARAGE.

Well if it isn't The Fast and the Furious*!* (A.J.)

Who said that? (Logan.)

Who said that? (A.J., mocking him.)

Seriously, who? (Logan.)

Seriously, who? (A.J., mocking him again.)

Let's get out of here. (Octavia.)

Pump the brakes, Blondie. (A.J.) *You're busted.*

Why? What did I do? (Octavia.)

Grand theft auto. (A.J.)

It wasn't theft. Sheridan Spencer gave me the keys and it's her dad's dealership so— (Octavia.)

It's true. (Logan.)

Don't bring Sheridan into this. (A.J.)

Um, I just did. (Octavia.)

Well, don't. (A.J.)

Why not? (Octavia.)

A.J. said his brain stopped beating when she said that because he didn't know how to respond. I didn't want to tell him that brains don't beat because some doctor might discover that they do beat and then I'd be the idiot.

A.J. said he told Octavia that he had a video of the whole

thing. And if she brought Sheridan into it he'd turn it over to the authorities.

And if I don't bring Sheridan into this? (Octavia.)

You walk. (A.J.)

Yes! Let's go. (Logan.)

Not you. Just the girl. (A.J.) *You have to confess to Mr. Spencer so I can get my job back.*

Sounds fair. (Octavia.)

It does not! (Logan.)

You drove. (Octavia.)

You gave me the keys. (Logan.)

I got them from Sher— (Octavia.)

Hey! Leave her out of it. (A.J.)

Oops. (Octavia.)

Do we have a deal? (A.J.)

Works for me. (Octavia, right before she bolted.)

Now Logan is in Dad's office confessing. And thanks to A.J.'s beating brain, I'm not.

END FLASHBACK.

SHERIDAN presses her ear against the door.

This is what I hear: Mumble...mumble...I'm not looking to ruin anyone's future...That's a relief...mumble...laughter...Logan, you could have been in an accident...Or worse...Logan mumbles something...silence...Mr. Pratt says something about the Noble Country Club...Best golf course in the Tristate...Five-year waiting list...and something about Logan being a great caddy. Dad says he likes

68

the sound of that...He doesn't sound angry anymore...Mr. Pratt asks if they have a deal...Dad mumbles...Logan says, THANK YOU, SIR!

Footsteps.

They're coming.

To Be Continued...

END SCENE.

Jagger

Oct. 21.

Audri goes to stay at her dad's for the weekend. Before she leaves she says she's going to miss me. Then she asks me to stay in touch.

LIE #21: How? Street urchins like me don't exactly have phones.

Turns out that lie should have come with a warning label. Side effects may include: sudden loss of Audri, severe Audri withdrawal, and feeling like those Central Park horses that are forced to wear blinders. Because not communicating with Audri for an entire weekend is like not being allowed to see.

I know she is somewhere in Montclair. But the rest? Like who she's hanging with, if she misses me, what time she's been going to bed, what she is wearing... Blind.

The only thing I do know is that she'll be home at 6 PM.

LIE #22: I just so happen to be biking on Vaji Boulevard at 5:59 PM.

Mr. Dunsing drops her off at 6:02 PM.

He asks Audri if she wants him to stay until her mom gets home.

Audri says no. It's okay. Her friend Jagger will wait with her.

I smile like the word "friend" doesn't sting.

Audri invites me inside.

Her living room isn't all tidy like mine. The blankets on the couch aren't folded into crisp triangles. They're in a heap. Crumpled-up girl magazines are all over the coffee table. Pages of models have been torn out and dropped onto the rug. There's a smudged flat-screen above the fireplace. It's the kind of fireplace that turns on with a key. I tell Audri it's the kind of place that makes me want to eat a huge plate of Hot Pockets and watch a *Shark Tank* marathon.

It's not *that* great, she says.

Let's agree to disagree, I say. Because I think it's perfect.

And it smells like roses. Maybe because there are vases of them everywhere.

Audri bets they're from Wreck-It Ralph. That's what she calls the guy who wrecked her parents' marriage. She knows he's still in the picture even though her mom swears he's not because who goes out and buys herself a billion roses?

LIE #23: I say no one, even though Mother did that to make Father jealous so he'd propose.

Audri says I can sit on the couch if I want.

I do.

She asks if I want a Coke.

LIE #24: Sure.

I really don't because Coke makes me burp but I don't want to tell her that, so . . .

We're looking through an IKEA catalogue to find Swedish names for Wreck-It Ralph.

I say Frykantig.

She counters with Sparsam.

We agree on Knutstorp.

We're laughing pretty hard when the inside pocket of my coat rings.

I freeze. I sweat. I take a long sip of soda.

Audri looks at me.

It rings again.

Q: Is that a phone?
A: Surprise!

— I thought you were a street urchin.

LIE #25: Randy got it for me. He's expecting a new shipment of exotic pets and wants to be able to reach me so I can help him unload.

Audri asks if Randy is getting any sugar gliders.
LIE #26: Yes.

Q: What's with you and sugar gliders, anyway?
A: For one thing they're even cuter than mice, and they fly.

Q: Isn't that two things?

Audri flicks my arm.
LIE #27: Ouch!
I pretend it hurts so I can flick her back.
Then it's kind of awkward for a minute so we both take sips of Coke.
Did you know that sugar gliders are extremely social, Audri says. Like if they don't get enough love they die.
I have to burp. I close my mouth and shoot the gas out my nostrils. It stings so bad my eyes water.
Audri thinks I'm tearing up because sugar gliders are so tragically sweet. I say she's my sugar glider. Audri says I'm hers.
I need her to clarify. Am I your "sugar glider" or your "friend"? I make those stupid air quotes so she knows I'm talking about the way she introduced me to her dad.
She smiles all crookedly and then asks what I want to be.
— Sugar glider.
— Good.
LIE #28: I'll ask Randy to save the cutest one for you.
Audri gives me a vanilla-scented hug.
Next thing I know we're baking trout.

73

Everything is a blurry mix of sensations so I can't even say who made the first move.

It's like my brain turned off and something else turned on. Only that something doesn't speak English. It doesn't register normal objects or sounds. It's a foreign language and I don't understand it. But my body does.

And it likes it.

A lot.

Lily

Sunday, October 21, 2012

Why, yes, Ms. Silver, the brown smear on this page is almond butter. How very astute of you. Please know that my decision to use this journal as a napkin was not meant to disrespect this assignment. I seriously never thought I'd be writing in it again. For I, Lily Bader-Huffman, had gone back to being a Homie.

For the past week, I've allowed my hair to embrace its natural frizz and have encouraged my T-zone to shine. I still watch Duffy from my window, but have redirected the time I spent trying to impress him toward bonding with the old crew. I feel like me again. The only downsides have been Maple's trick eye, which has gone from lazy to utterly listless, and Blake.

I've left him several messages—six to be exact—and he

hasn't called back. Knowing Blake, he's mad that I left him at Pub, which is so selfish because I'm the one who got yanked. Hence another reason I have embraced being a Homie. No more drama.

Unless you count the tiff I got into with Wendi over my new CNN anchor crush.

"You can't switch from Wolf Blitzer to Anderson Cooper," she said.

"Why not?" I asked.

"Anderson Cooper is gay!"

"So? That doesn't mean I can't like him."

"What's the point, Sisyphus?" she asked. "He'll never like you back."

I wanted to say, "I can't control who I like. If I could I wouldn't be spending my love dollars on Duffy, and Vanessa wouldn't be spending hers on Blake." But I didn't want to think about the things I've been trying to forget, so I said, "You're right. Maybe I am wasting my time on Anderson Cooper. So, how are things going with you and Sanjay Gupta? Has he responded to your nine-page letter?"

Wendi laughed and said it was good to have me back. I agreed. It was good to have me back.

That was my mind-set as I listened to Haim and prepped my study calendar for week two as a Homie v. 2.0.

Yes, I, Lily Bader-Huffman, was 95 percent happy. The missing 5 percent rested on Blake's cold shoulder but I knew he'd warm eventually. Pub or not, I was still his best friend.

Then I heard the knock.

"Lily," Dad said, "can we come in?"

We? I turned off the music.

For once, Dad led the way and Mom lingered in the doorway.

"I've made a terrible mistake," he sighed.

"Better you than me."

He sat on the edge of my desk. "I shouldn't have pulled you out of Noble."

"Wait, *what?*"

"It was wrong and I'm sorry. We've arranged to send you back."

I looked at Mom. She looked at the carpet.

"It's okay," I said. "You were right to pull me out. I'm doing better now."

"That's the problem," Dad said.

"Huh?"

"Lily!" Mom snapped.

"Sorry. I mean, excuse me, Dad? I don't understand."

Mom sighed and said, "We're doing you a disservice by continuing to homeschool you. Dad thinks you should learn from your mistakes, mistakes we're not giving you a chance to make."

"What does that even mean?"

"It means if you want to get bad grades you can," Dad said.

I looked at Mom. "Is he serious?"

She nodded yes.

"Your mother has given you a fantastic education. Her job

is done. What you do with that knowledge should be up to you now. Do you want to skip a few grades? Stay where you are and get straight A's? Fail? You're old enough and certainly smart enough to decide."

My bottom lip started to twitch.

"What your father's trying to say, Lil, is that we can't keep protecting you."

"Protecting me from what?"

"From yourself," she said. "It's your future. You have to be responsible for it."

"What about what I want?"

"This is what you wanted," Dad said. "You wrote an entire essay about the benefits of going to Noble."

"That was before!"

"Before what?"

"Before I went to Noble."

Mom slid a finger under her glasses and wiped a tear from her eye. I didn't feel the least bit sorry for her. I despised her for agreeing to something she clearly didn't support.

"The plan was to homeschool you for six years," she said, "after which I'd return to my psychology practice. Then six turned into eight because I didn't want to let you go. But your father's right, Lily. It's time."

Self-pity pooled in my eyes. I blinked, forcing my tears into the world to make their own mistakes; a world that will wipe them away because they don't belong.

"So you're breaking up with me?" I asked.

"Please," Mom said. "We'll be here for you every step of the way."

"Oh," I snapped. "So you're breaking up with me but you want to stay friends."

Mom turned to Dad. "See, Alan! I told you this was wrong."

"Lily!" Dad said. "We are not breaking up with you." Then to Mom, "It's not easy, Nora, but it's not wrong!"

Mom turned and walked out. Dad went after her. And I, Lily Bader-Huffman, was left alone.

Lily Bader-Huffman-Duffy

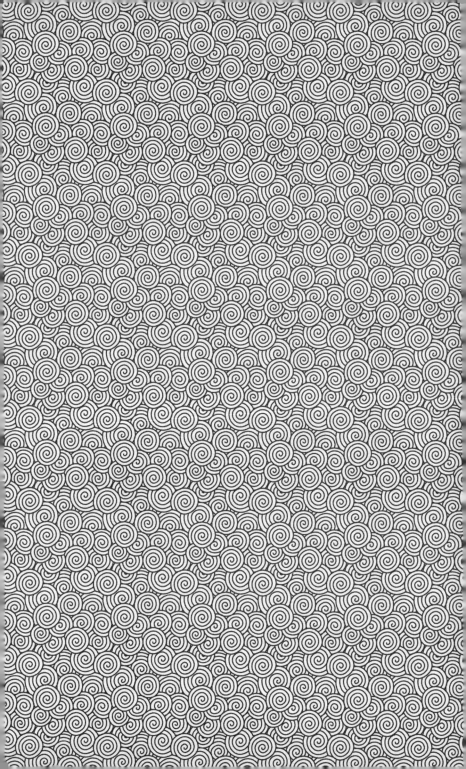

Lily

Monday, October 22, 2012

I couldn't do it. Blake is still sending me to voice mail and I didn't want to walk in alone. Everyone would ask why I'm back. Or why I left in the first place. Or worse—what if they didn't even notice I was gone?

I didn't know how to deal with any of those scenarios. So even though I wasn't talking to Mom, I told her I had Coxsackie. I didn't care what she thought. I didn't care about anything but *not* going to Noble.

"I guess you'd better stay home," Mom said.

"You believe me?"

"Why shouldn't I?"

"Do you even know what Coxsackie is?"

"A virus. Symptoms include a sore throat, rash, and blisters in the mouth."

Of course she knew.

"And you believe I have those symptoms?"

"No."

"Then why are you letting me stay home?"

"It's your life," she said. "Your grades, your future." She kissed me on the forehead, hooked her purse over her shoulder, and headed down the hall.

I followed her.

"That's it? That's all you're going to say?"

"That's it." She opened the front door. It was raining again.

"Where are you going?"

"To buy a pack of gum."

"You're going out in the rain for *gum*?"

Mom shrugged. "It's a start." She smiled at the ridiculousness of it all, but I also detected a hint of pride in her expression. Whether she was leaving for gum or a job interview was beside the point. The point was she was leaving, whether she was ready to or not.

I wanted to smile too, but I refused to give her the satisfaction.

So now I'm back in bed. Journaling and eating almond butter.

It's a start.

Lily Bader-Huffman-Duffy

DUFFY

Monday

I'm waiting for Sheridan outside the theater. They're practicing a song. It's about being popular. I should probably take notes.

Trying to fill these pages. Trying. Trying. Try. Ing. Tryi. Ng.

Ng. Ng. Ng. Ng.

There was a guy who used to work for Dad before he was in the red and had to close the real estate office. His name was Edwin Nguyen. I thought it was Edwin N-gooyin. But he said Ng is pronounced like a W. I asked what it was like having a name like Edwin Win cuz I was pretty sure it had to suck. He thought about it for a second then said: It's a win-win.

I kind of laughed but I also felt like bawling my eyes out.

The guy had no clue how tragic he was. Wait, let me rewrite that. The guy had no clue how tragic he Ngas.

I wish Ms. Silver let us journal on computers. Copy. Paste. Copy. Paste. Copy. Paste. Copy. Paste. Command C. Command V. Command C. Command V. DONE!

I guess I could write about how my entire life has changed since Saturday. Only it's hard to sit still.

Feeling = I'd rather live my changed life than write about it. But Sheridan won't be done for another twenty minutes and I don't want to look like a guy who has nothing better to do than wait.

The last thing I wrote about was Trendemic. I was trying to pick things to sell but all I could think about was Coach Bammer and how he'd kick me where the balls don't bounce if I missed scrimmage. So I clicked the first seven things I saw that didn't ooze slickness and bolted. I don't even remember what I chose.

I was the first one in the gym. I thought Bammer would be so impressed he'd change his mind and let me play. All he did was point to the bench and say: Warm it.

When the rest of the team showed up and saw me sitting, the nicknames started flying. They called me Bleacher Creature, Dame Judi Bench, and Hairy Penal. Penal was short for penalized. Hairy was just an add-on.

The unfunny jokes came next.

Q: What did the bench say when he was introduced to Duffy's butt?
A: Pleasure to seat you.

Q: Why did Duffy get kicked off the Flames?
A: He didn't give a sit.

Knock knock.
Who's there?
Duffy.
Duffy who?
Exactly.
Feeling = I wish I was the Incredible Hulk.

My Flames shirt would rip open and I'd get huge. Then I'd lift the bench over my head and snap it in half like a carrot. They'd scream and try to run away. I'd scoop them up and jam them in the nets. Their dangling legs would bicycle in midair. The backboards would crack. The hoops would start to give. Coach Bammer would beg me to show them mercy. He'd say they didn't mean anything by it. They were just being guys and that's what guys do. They razz.

I'd lower myself down, look him in the eyes, and burp that stupid word right back in his face. RAAAAAAAAA AAAAAAAAAAAAAAZZZZZZZZZ ZZZ.

Bammer would fix his burp-blown hair and then offer me captain but only if I saved them. I'd tap my green chin like I was mulling it over. Meanwhile, the backboards would give even more. Bammer would start begging. I'd keep tapping. And right when everyone started to fall, I'd swoop in and catch them.

Then, as their new captain, I'd give them three minutes to change their shorts. They'd thank me as they ran toward the locker room covering their butts in shame.

Feeling = How awesome would that be?

Anyway, I didn't need to do that. Logan Pratt is off the Flames for stealing the BMW. His dad wants him to be a caddy or some crap. That's what Bammer said. Exactly like that. So I'm back in the game!

I can't wait to tell Sheridan.

—LATER

Sheridan

10.22.12

INT. FRONT SEAT OF THE BMW M5—LATE AFTERNOON.

SHERIDAN would rather put quill to paper in
a vehicle that smells like graham crackers than
follow MOM and the TWINS around REI. HENRY and
MAX need soccer cleats. They get whatever they
want. SHERIDAN does not.

Call me Big Game Hunting because I am channeling a bad
sport. I can't help it. Everyone's dreams come true but mine. A
starring role would be the ultimate, but right now I'd settle for
playing the lead in someone's life. Audri has clearly replaced
me with Jagger. According to today's lunch letter they had an

"epic make-out" on Sunday and are officially boyfriend and girlfriend. They even call each other sugar gliders.

(Barf.)

O'course I "acted" superlatively happy for Audri. Only I didn't feel happy. I felt like her hormones skipped a grade and made all new friends. Meanwhile, I got my period one month before she did. So if anyone should be "epically making out" it should be me because my body matured twenty-eight days before Audri's. But hooking up is not trending with me right now.

I don't really know how. How did Audri? If there's a script, I certainly haven't seen it.

I hoped to get the details after rehearsal but she was busy helping Octavia gather her things. Yes, Journal, you heard me right. I said, Audri was *helping* Octavia. Why did Octavia need help, you ask? Because Octavia claims she got whiplash from joyriding with Logan and needs "Owdie" to be her "nurse."

SOLILOQUY.

Funny, Octavia, A.J. didn't mention anything about you getting hurt. In fact, he said you ran off pretty quickly and left Logan behind to take all the blame. But you'll do anything to keep Audri and me apart, won't you? Well, you're not the only one who can manipulate my best friend! I'll invite Audri and Jagger on a double date with Duffy and me. Rosco's, table for four! No more joiners. Move over, whiplash, a new pain in the neck just rolled into town. Her name is Sheridan Spencer and she's gonna make you suffer.

END OF SOLILOQUY.

CUT TO:

Duffy was in the hall when I got out of rehearsal. He was sitting all sweaty and flushed from practice, writing in his journal. Suddenly I became jealous of his pen, like it was some flirty girl or something, because it knew his secrets and I didn't. I knew better than to ask what he was writing about. It was none of my business. Our journals were private and everyone knew it. Anyway, if he wanted to tell me he would.

What are you writing about? (Me, not being able to help it.)

Just trying to fill pages. He closed the journal, dropped it in his backpack, and zipped it up. FYI—he never zips his backpack. So now I'm curious with a side of paranoid. But I have to let it go. I have to be cool. I can't give in to—

Fill the pages with what? (Me, not letting it go, not being cool, and giving in.)

He looked at me kind of sideways and said, *Words.*

I had to let it go. I had to change the subject. I blurt-asked him if he wanted to go on a double date. Only I called it a double hang because I didn't want him to think I was looking for a sugar glider.

Cool. (Duffy.)

Okay, cool. (Me, hoping Audri and Jagger would agree.)

Instead of busting out iCal and making it official, Duffy changed the subject to basketball. Turns out that after meeting with my dad, Mr. Pratt made Logan quit the Flames as part of his punishment. Which means Duffy's bench-warming days are over. He's back on the team and the best part is he'll never have to deal with Logan again. I didn't want to be all Robert Downer Jr. and ruin his moment so I forced my outsides to look happy for him. But my insides were *très Les Misérables*. Now Duffy will go back to being a star and I'll be left behind, again, waiting in the wings.

He asked if I wanted to celebrate with a frozen hot chocolate from the Honey Bun. I said I couldn't because of this whole cleat shopping thing. But really? This fading star has lost her twinkle. Not that I'm incapable of feeling joy for others. I can. As long as I feel more joy for myself. And right now the only thing I feel is FADE TO BLACK.

To Be Continued...

END SCENE.

DUFFY

Tuesday

Hud and Coops used to call my house the Playboy Mansion. They probably still would if they were speaking to me. But they aren't.

Feeling = I bet they would if I really did live at the Playboy Mansion.

Feeling = How sick would that be?

Anyway, it's like they think Mandy comes home from school, takes off her clothes, and dances around in underwear all night with Megan and Morgan. Coops calls it the pants-off dance-off.

Feeling = More like the turn-off dance-off.

Thinking about my sister in her underwear is like matching up two south poles of a magnet. Force it all you want but it's never gonna work. With Megan and Morgan it's different. Sort of. I'm not related to them so they could do a pants-off dance-off and it wouldn't repel me. But their filibustering does.

I learned that word today in American Politics. I thought it had something to do with bras, but a filibuster is a professional time waster.

Like say the Democrats are playing against the Republicans for some legislation. Republicans are ahead 22–18 in the final quarter. With ten minutes to go, the Republicans send in a ringer—some slick dude whose whole job is to talk and talk and talk until the buzzer goes so the Dems can't score. That ringer is a filibuster.

Feeling = Amelia would kill me for saying this because it's disrespectful toward women, but girls are natural-born filibusters.

Feeling = Especially Mandy, Morgan, and Megan. They're in the kitchen. I'm in the den. I can hear everything. They may as well be wearing Bubbie Libby's flannel nightgowns and mint arthritis cream. Their conversation is that un-hot.

Feeling = I want to block their bustering with noise-canceling headphones and some Kings of Leon. But I'll transcribe what they're saying instead. For one thing, if Hud and Coops ever talk to me again I'm going to make them read it. And for another, dialogue takes up journal space and I'm way behind on pages.

MEGAN: Ohmygod will someone please take these Snapea Crisps away from me. I'm about to finish the whole bag.

MORGAN: I know, right? They're so yum.

MANDY: *Soooo* yum!

MORGAN: Right?

MEGAN: Crazy. (Chewing.) Who told you about them?

MANDY: *SELF* magazine. Or maybe it was *Shape*. I dunno. One of them.

MORGAN: Swear they're healthy?

MANDY: They're snap peas! (Silence.) *What?* Why are you looking at me like that?

MORGAN: You're not eating any.

MANDY: I'm full. I downed a ton of Persian cucumbers at lunch.

MORGAN: Those make you lose weight and you know it.

MEGAN: They do?

MORGAN: Given! They have like, zero grams of everything so chewing actually burns calories.

MANDY: Same with Snapea Crisps, right?

MORGAN: Doubt it. Megan, fact-check please.

MEGAN: 150 calories.

MORGAN: Serving size?

MEGAN: 22 pieces.

MORGAN: Fat grams?

MEGAN: 8.

MORGAN: Mandeee!

MANDY: Yikes. That's high.

MORGAN: Sodium?

MEGAN: 125 mg.

MORGAN: Seriously?

(Sound of crisps being dumped into the sink. Then the garbage disposal.)

MEGAN: Ohmygod, I'm going to look like Erin Applegate!

MORGAN: (Sings like LMFAO.) *There's a carb-face in the house tonight / Everybody just have a good time . . .*

(Laughter.)

MANDY: It's not carb-face. She's on steroids. Hashtag ulcer. You heard it here first.

MEGAN: Sucks.

MORGAN: Poor thing.

MEGAN: Right?

MORGAN: Ugh.

MANDY: Highlight-delete the pity. That girl was a Phoenix Five. She got early acceptance to Yale and Princeton. If anyone should have an ulcer, it's me. I only have two AP classes, one after-school job, and four extracurriculars. I'll be lucky to get into McDonald's College. Hashtag HamburgerUniversity.

MEGAN: At least you have Gardner. I've been single for three weeks.

MORGAN: Try five! Soon to be five hundred, thanks to those snap peas.

Feeling = I swear, I'm about to Van Gogh my ears off. I don't care how hot you are. Any girl who bad-mouths a snack while it's still in her mouth can't be trusted. Sheridan eats whatever and doesn't filibuster about it. It's cool.

She asked if I wanted to grab a bite with Audri and Jagger on Thursday. We'll probably end up at Rosco's because everyone goes there after school, including my entire team. Maybe if Hud and Coops see me hanging out with new people they'll realize how much they miss me and they'll take me back.

I just put on my headphones. Blasting "Sex on Fire."

Feeling = Kings need a new album. I've listened to *Only by the Night* six hundred times this week.

Feeling = I need friends.

—LATER

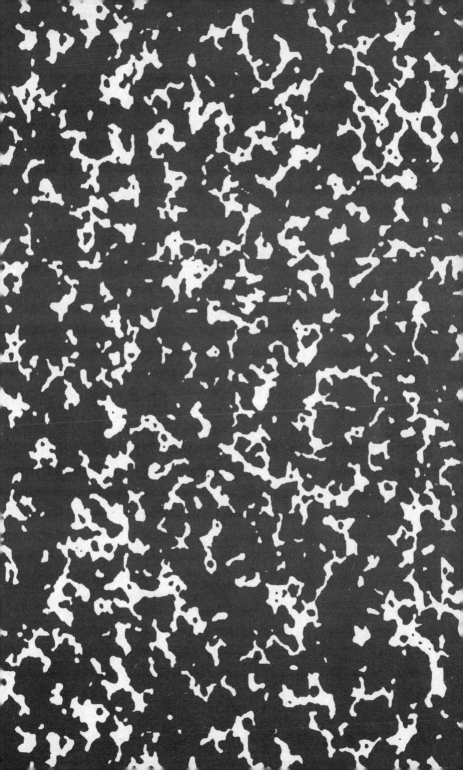

Jagger

Oct. 24.

Audri and I baked trout by the bike rack before first period this morning.

The tip of her nose was cold. Her tongue tasted like a candy cane.

I thought of that blond girl from the Orbit gum commercial. Only for a second and only because she reminds me of frost.

We kept at it until some jerk yelled, "Get a room!"

I removed my lips from her face. Not to Google "rooms in Noble, NJ" or anything.

LIE #29: But because "get a room" is such an unoriginal thing to say. Like, "thank god it's Friday" or "chillax." And predictability turns me off.

That's what I told Audri. Better that than admitting I was scared we'd get caught baking trout on campus. Scared my parents would get called to the principal's office. Scared I'd have to explain why two death row inmates rolled up in a red Mercedes coupe, Ralph Lauren wardrobes, and Caribbean suntans.

Then Audri says, wanna know what turns me off?

So I say, sure.

Liars.

LIE #30: Me too.

Lily

Wednesday, October 24, 2012

Day One at Pub v. 2.0.

My first day back at Noble had me feeling like a fart: invisible and off-putting.

Correction. Off-putting implies that I mattered enough to be offensive. I didn't. I was on the wrong side of popular when my parents pulled me out; now I'm not even important enough to bully.

The moment I entered the locker zone Blake walked off with Vanessa. I managed to hold back my tears by telling myself he didn't see me. But that became harder to believe after he blustered past me. Twice. I swear, he moved so fast I felt wind. The worst part? It's been a week and I still can't figure out why he's ignoring me. Is it because:

a) I accidentally took his English binder, costing him a paltry 10 percent on his homework?

b) I was involuntarily removed from Pub and inadvertently left him behind?

c) The nonstop rain is doing nothing for his olive skin and he needs someone to blame?

The Homies strongly believe it's b) because they're convinced Blake is in love with me. If only I could say they have me confused with someone more male, perhaps I'd be further along in this investigation. But Captain Closet won't let me. So their input was useless.

By lunch I was desperate and decided to try the one thing—besides the slightest mention of Coxsackie—guaranteed to make Blake laugh. I crept up behind him and placed a Baked Lay ever-so-gently on his shoulder. Faster than I could say, "Why is there a chip on your shoulder?" he crushed it in his fist and shook the crumbs on the floor. He didn't even bother turning around.

Should you ever wonder what "dead" feels like, put a Baked Lay on your best friend's shoulder and watch him pretend it's not funny. You could also wave to the only boy you've ever loved (besides the fictional Seth Cohen from *The O.C.*), then smile expectantly while he does NOT wave back.

Still not feeling adequately deceased? Join the Noble High style club, then leave school for six days. When you return to discover you've been replaced by Brianna Plume because she too "has a flair for European androgyny" and "someone said you died," you'll feel it. Believe me, you will.

Eight years of straight A's and social sacrifice for what? I'm nothing but a Homie without a home. A friendless phenom. A Pub-fart.

Sure, intellectual superiority counts for something, but not enough. Ask anyone who's ever graduated what they remember most about high school. Actually, don't bother. I'll tell you. They remember their first kiss. First date. First love. Best friends. Winning goal. Prom.

Not Calculus. Not History or Biology or AP English.

So scrape the rose-colored tint off your glasses, America, and take an honest look at what it *really* means to succeed in high school. Good grades, you say?

Ha! I say.

If grades mattered, I, Lily Bader-Huffman, would be Noble royalty. Those checkerboard tiles would be my catwalk. Teachers, my butt-kissing sponsors. Students, my entourage. I'd need a twenty-four-hour security detail. I'd be paid to design school supplies for Target. I'd be Phoenix one, two, three, four, and five. I'd still miss out on being a typical teen. But in this scenario I'd accept my fate more willingly. Because I would no longer be a silent but deadly Pub-fart.

I, Lily Bader-Huffman, would be seen.

Lily Bader-Huffman-Duffy

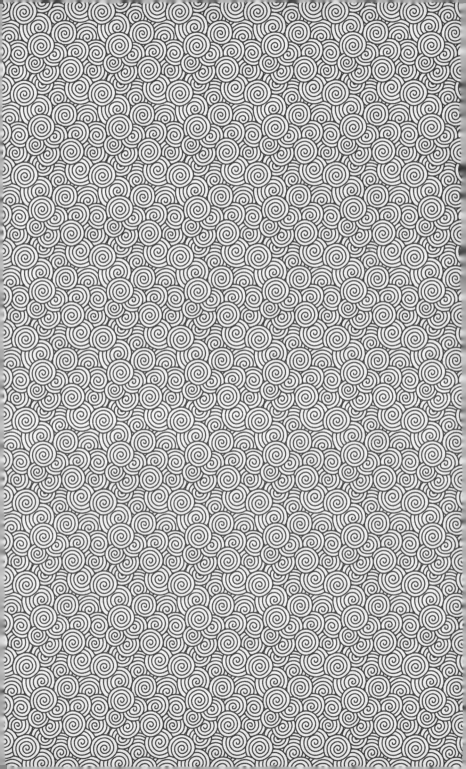

Vanessa

October 24th

Dad's favorite band is named... wait for it... *The Band*.[70] Ver. I'm not making that up. Anyway, they have this song called "Life Is a Carnival." The last time I heard it we were driving upstate to go apple picking. That was two years ago. The fighting wasn't so bad back then. Nothing was.

"Kids," Dad said, eyeballing A.J. and me in the rearview mirror. "If life really was a carnival, what would you be?"

"Owner!" I called.

....

[70] I know, really creative, right? Are the members named Singer, Guitarist, Drummer, and Bassist?

"Kissing booth," Mom announced.

Gross, A.J. mouthed.

Dad rubbed his stubble and in his best falsetto said, "I'd be the bearded lady."

"Fun house," A.J. said.

"Yes. Yes, you would," Mom said. I swear I could hear her smiling.

If we had that conversation today, A.J. would be an upside-down roller coaster, Mom would be half woman, half fire-breathing dragon, and Dad would be the barker.

Me? I'd be Whac-A-Mole because right when I solve one problem, another pops up.

The latest, which also happens to be my greatest, is Lily. If life was a carnival, Lily would own the deed to the land. Just as I was starting to make a profit she'd show up and shut me down.

Competing with her for grades *and* Blake is completely demoralizing. Both come so naturally to her. So you can imagine my relief when she, like a blister, was lanced from my life.

Lily's swift removal upgraded me to *smartest female freshman* after only three days of tenacious classroom participation and intimidating posture. It also gave Blake an unobstructed view of me, which in turn eliminated my need to humble-brag.

Noble became so unequivocally rewarding my arms stopped itching at school. Mom's been working late now that Dad's back from the tech convention, so there hasn't been much conflict at home either. Like, none. Today I wore my short-sleeved blouse with the flouncy bow.[71] Normally, I might have humble-bragged with something like, "The crossing guard told me my shirt was the same blue as my eyes. But my eyes are emerald green. Do you think he's color blind?"

Only I didn't have to.

First thing this morning, Blake stopped by my locker. He wanted to know if I had seen Jagger and Audri's colossal make-out session by the bike stand.

"Jagger is getting some satisfaction," I said. His expression changed from delight to confusion. My arms began to tingle. "You know that Rolling Stones song?" I clasped my hands behind my back to keep from scratching. "Sorry, I'm corny sometimes. I get it from my dad."

"No," Blake said, fanning away my apology. "It's that color. It's great on you. Honestly? I can't tell where that blouse ends and your eyes begin. Hurry, you take a selfie while I alert Pantone."

Giggling, I drew my hair over my left shoulder, thusly accentuating my "good side." I held the phone at a forty-five-degree angle to capture my scratch-free arms, then angled my face toward the light. I was close to locking in the shot when Blake said, "Uh-oh."

I followed his gaze to the front doors, where the sun had cast a yolk-colored parallelogram on the checkered floor. There stood a girl. She was backlit but her silhouette was unmistakable. Wild hair, loping gait, skateboard tucked inside

....

[71] *Très* Paris street style and did I mention short-sleeved?

her armpit; either Shaun White had transferred to Noble High or the blister was back.

Of all the questions running through my mind, only one required my immediate attention. Now what? Staying meant scratching. But if I left, Lily would occupy Blake Street and kick me to the curb.

Thankfully, I didn't have to choose. Blake grabbed me by the itchy arm and dragged me away.

The itching should have ended there, but as a habitual competitor and former captain of the eighth-grade track-and-field team, I knew that if I wanted to stay in first position I had to fight harder than ever. I had to stay focused on my goals and not let Lily or her former, albeit flawless, track record intimidate me. I had to put some serious distance between us. I had to apply the 10 percent rule.

Yesterday, during warm-up, Coach Speedman said the smartest way for a runner to increase her speed is to increase her efforts by 10 percent each week. Anything more could cause injury or burnout, and anything less wouldn't be enough. In other words, if I work 10 percent smarter[72] than Lily each week I will always stay 10 percent ahead.

Increasing my study time by one hour per subject was the obvious way to improve my performance in class. But I was struggling with the Blake aspect. Lily had years of history with him. Six days of lunches and hallway banter couldn't possibly

---

[72] Smarter + Harder = Smarder

compete with that. Humble-bragging was an option, but I want courting, not campaigning. I want everyone to marvel at how fetching we look together. I want to be the first couple in Noble history to be part of the Phoenix Five. I want to apply to the same colleges, somewhere far away from the fighting.

Ver? I want to believe that love can still be done. I want what Audri and the Orphan have. I want to Blake-out.[73]

You can fly off a mountaintop if anybody can.

—The Band, "Life Is a Carnival"

---

[73] I need to humble-brag about this term.

DUFFY

Wednesday

Like two seconds after I got home from school the bell rang. I opened the door but no one was there. Just a black box from Trendemic. There were seven things inside. Eight if you count the death threat from Anton.

It Guy #71470,

Bloody noses are red,

Violence is blue,

Pay me back by December 1, 2012

Or you will regret it big-time.

(So will your face.)

—Anton Pryce, Style Sensei/Debt Collector

In other words, I have thirty-seven days to find $2,074.00. I am supposed to do it by selling these things:

1. <u>WhispHer for Him</u>: A seductive body spray made from the sweat glands of German stud horses. Dry and woodsy with hints of vanilla and dark chocolate. Guaranteed to attract women. ($12.95) Coming soon: <u>DenHim for Her</u>.

2. <u>The Calm Dome</u>: A wool beanie with built-in scalp massager. ($9.75)

3. <u>Heavy Metal Bands</u>: Now you can sweat in style. Gold cuff bracelets lined with moisture-wicking terry cloth. ($19.25/pair)

4. <u>The Girlfriend Sweater</u>: A rugged cable-knit sweater with a single side pocket so your girl has a place to warm her hand while you stroll arm in arm. ($36.00)

5. <u>The Love Glove</u>: For the couple that can't let go, these gloves have been specially designed to fit two hands. ($15.75)

6. <u>Toolery</u>: Like a Swiss Army knife, this silver ring contains seven flip-up tools guaranteed to turn every boy into an alpha male. ($24.99)

7. <u>Electrick Jeans</u>: Loose fit with a back pocket that charges your smartphone. ($39.99)

I'm supposed to wear these slick embarrassments, wait for a bunch of suckers to compliment me, then tell them how they too can dress like a Brookstone mannequin. My mission is to make them believe I'd rock this look even if my life didn't depend on it.

Feeling = I wouldn't.

I searched the Trendemic box one last time before I tossed it. I was looking for my soul. No luck. Anton still has it.

— LATER

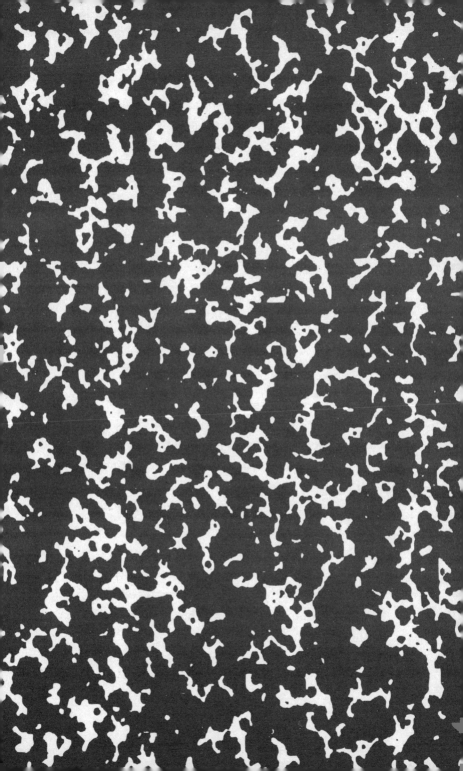

Jagger

Oct. 25.

Audri and I are a "thing" and everyone knows it.

It's obvious because no one talks to us when we're together. We get plenty of closed-mouth smiles and wassup head nods but no one actually stops and hangs.

Audri says it's a respect thing.

Like we're mobsters? I ask.

— No. They respect the bubble and don't want to infiltrate it.

— What bubble?

— The lo-like bubble. It's invisible but people know it's there.

— Huh?

— Think of it as a cage for sugar gliders.

I say, ahhh, like a dude who suddenly gets it.

LIE #31: I don't.

I don't even care. My insides are dinging and flashing like a pinball machine because Audri meant to say *love*-like bubble.

She knows it too. She's blushing and the body doesn't lie. The brain does, though.

It can't help itself. Lies infest it like termites. They come in droves and mow the cerebral cortex like some all-you-can-eat buffet. Soon it's all holes and droppings where the truth used to be.

I'm already mostly holes and droppings so I can pretend I don't hear the "lo" part. Not because I'm afraid to go there with Audri. I'm not. But because walking to Rosco's with Sheridan and Duffy is not when you want to admit you're in lo-like.

Or that you don't know jack about double dates.

All I know is that Duffy and Sheridan are kind of a thing and Audri and I are kind of a thing and since Audri and Sheridan are a thing we're supposed to start doing things together.

So there we are. Jammed around the hostess podium waiting for a table. A few guys from the Flames are ahead of us. They see Duffy but don't say hi.

I assume it's because he's with me and they know I'm a Ponnowitz. But they haven't figured that out yet so that can't be it.

Then I get it.

They know he's in a lo-like bubble with Sheridan and they're showing respect.

But Brandy the hostess? She couldn't care less. She pokes her nose right through it and takes a big sniff of Duffy's neck.

She says he smells crazy-good.

Like a chocolate bonfire.

Whatever that means.

Then she goes, mmmmmm.

Meanwhile Sheridan just stands there looking all proud. Now that's confidence.

If some waiter poked through my lo-like bubble to sniff Audri, I'd stuff his nostrils with those pee-covered mints by the cash register.

Anyway, the guys on the Flames are staring because Brandy is being kind of loud with her *mmmmm*s, and of the entire Rosco's staff she's the blondest.

Then she goes, if my boyfriend smelled like you I wouldn't have dumped him. What is that?

It's WhispHer for Him, Duffy says. Go to Trendemic.com and enter the code #71470 for a special discount. You didn't hear it from me.

The guy is suave. I'll give him that.

Jagger is not one for high-maintenance grooming but when a girl loses it for a dude's neck smell it doesn't matter who you're pretending to be. You want that neck smell for yourself. So instead of entering Trendemic.com #71470 on my phone like some of the other eavesdroppers, I memorize it. Because cologne is not the kind of thing emancipated orphans spend their pennies on.

We sit and the girls go right into how excited they are that *The X Factor* got renewed for another season. I have nothing to say about that so I look around the place like I've never seen anyone serve fries before.

Then I need air.

For one thing, I'm all knee-to-knee with Duffy and I don't want him to think I'm okay with that because I'm not. For another thing, Audri is wearing her tennis skirt. The one with the J on it for good luck. My fake initial is so close to her thigh that my upper lip starts to sweat.

I tell her that.

LIE #32: Well, not all of it. Just the part about the initial and the thigh. Not the lip sweat.

Audri puts her hand on my knee. My upper lip floods. I fan my face with the menu. She asks if I'm okay.

— Yes, why?

Audri says I look like I've been sitting in front of an open dishwasher. I know she's talking about the steam that pours out when you open the door mid-cycle. But I'd never admit that, so I go, what's his name?

— Whose name? she asks.

— The dishwasher's.

This cracks everyone up and we forget I'm sweating. Next thing you know we're coming up with dishwasher names like Reese WitherSPOON (Sheridan), CLEAN Abdul-Jabbar (Duffy), RINSE William (Audri), and SOAP John Paul II (me).

Audri is laughing so hard her glasses fog. She wipes them on my Rolling Stones shirt.

I say it's no big deal. Wipe away. I got this shirt from the Goodwill. It was like fifty cents.

LIE #33: The shirt is vintage. It belonged to Georgia Jagger, Mick's daughter. Father was offered $1,500 for it by the Hard Rock Cafe. He said no.

I need to clean off Audri's lens residue before the value depreciates. I need to emancipate my knee from Duffy. I excuse myself from the booth.

LIE #34: I touched a gum wad under the table. Gotta wash my hands.

There's a 25¢ machine outside the bathroom. It's pushing scented erasers, sparkly key chains, rainbow stickers. That kind of thing.

I put in a quarter and turn. Out rolls a clear plastic ball. There's a purple ring inside. It says *Best Friend* in yellow bubble letters. I put it in the front pocket of my jeans. I want to give it to Audri when we are alone. To express my lo-like.

I go back to the table. Audri says they already ordered, then stands so I can slide back in. I'm knee-to-knee with Duffy again. He knows it's awkward and chexts. That's my sugar glider's made-up word for checking texts. Chexting.

If any other girl ever said gimme a minute while I chext, I'd give her more than a minute. I'd give her an eternity. But Audri makes it work.

The Flames sit across from us. They're looking at us and laughing. Duffy is chexting and doesn't notice. My nervous system does.

My pits itch.

My intestines beat like a heart.

The taste of Susan B. Anthony dollars fills my mouth.

I move my knee as far away from Duffy's as possible: one-eighth of an inch.

They yuk it up even harder.

If you've ever been looked at and laughed at for three years straight you know how real this is.

I try to remember what Dr. Lloyd taught me.

1) Get out of your head, Daniel.
2) Look around the room. Name five objects. Five colors. Five sounds.
3) It's just a panic attack. It will pass.

It does. The panic, I mean. Not the yukking up. So I rest my elbow on Audri's shoulder to prove I'm not getting bromantic on their teammate.

The desserts come. A lot of them.

Sheridan attacks the Oreo cheesecake.

She asks Duffy why he's staring at her.

He says because he never sees girls eat. Sheridan stops chewing but doesn't spit the cake out. It just sits there in her open mouth while she looks at Duffy and goes, is that a bad thing?

Duffy says, no way! It's the best. It means you have passion.

Smooth. No wonder girls sniff him.

Audri nuzzles her cheek into my arm. Her glasses poke into my flesh. I don't care.

She feeds me a bite of warm apple cobbler.

I feed her a spoonful of vanilla bean ice cream.

She feeds some back to me. It gets on my lip. She licks it off.

We bake trout.

Right there.

In front of everyone.

It's so tacky.

I don't care.

I can't stop.

That 25¢ plastic ball feels like it's going to burst through the front of my jeans and shoot clear across the room. I take it out and stuff it down the back of the booth.

The bill comes.

Audri says she has me covered because I barely ate anything. I know she's just trying to be nice because she thinks I'm poor. But I'm a liar, not a mooch, and insist on paying.

I pull a brown paper bag out of my backpack. It's filled with pennies. Rolls and rolls of them. I say I find them on the streets. Money is money.

LIE #35: There is an entire closet in the Legacy Hygienics Mini Mavericks club filled with penny rolls. Kids use them to make wishes in the koi ponds. I use them to make friends.

We're walking home. It's raining and dark and the streetlights glare like Paris. It's the perfect time to give her the lo-like ring. Only I forgot it in the booth.

So I give her a roll of pennies instead.

She says she loves them.

I say I love *her*.

She asks if I mean it.

I say yes.

She smiles. She says she loves me too. She makes me promise that I won't break her heart.

I promise.

LIE #36.

Sheridan

10.25.12

INT. THE SPENCER HOME—BATHROOM—NIGHT.

SHERIDAN locks the door, then turns to the looking glass to address her reflection. Correction:
her soul.

Mom says you seem angry at the world lately. Is that true?
(SHERIDAN to her caramel-colored eyes.) It's okay.
Take your time. Go deep...

BEAT.

Mom's accusation would be true if this was last month.
Because I'm angry at Audri and last month Audri was my
world. But not anymore. Do you hear that, soul? NOT. ANY.

MORE. Today's public display of affection was more like a public display of rejection. Toward me.

The whole point of the double hang was to get Audri away from Octavia so we could make new memories. Would I have preferred a one-on-one? O'course. But without the jaws of life there's no separating her and Jagger so I included him. I'm supportive like that. Another thing about me? I'd never compete against Audri for the Most Attention from a Boy award. But the second Duffy said I'm passionate she one-upped me with a make-out. As if *that's* passion. It's day-class-ay if you ask me!

Anyway, Audri, if that made you appear passionate I certainly didn't notice. I was too busy chexting messages I didn't have. My eyes needed to make an emergency landing on something before they crashed into Duffy. What if he thought I wanted to make out too? What if he thought I didn't? What if he heard what you told me when we were putting on our coats—that something of Jagger's was pressing against your leg while you were mauling each other?

Cheeses, Audri, did you not see Duffy getting smelt-up by that put-the-ho-in-hostess? Do you know how hard it is to channel a blind person when someone is doing that to your crush? Duffy is superlatively cute. He's on the Varsity team. He started wearing cologne!

DUFFY. HAS. OPTIONS!

And there you R (yes, it's a pun for rated R), reminding him—and half the guys on his team—that he's with a rated

PG (for Prude Girl). Yes, Audri, you took the R-bar, hooked it to a gigantic crane, and raised it high above my head. Duffy knows it, too. We haven't reached sugar glider status yet but the chemistry has been undeniable. We were getting there. Now, notsomuch. Look what he gave me!

SHERIDAN lifts her hand to the mirror. A purple plastic eyesore saying *Best Friend* comes into frame.

If this doesn't state-example-explain his intentions in perfect paragraph form (only with a ring instead of a paragraph), nothing will. What I wanted was to be his leading lady, but he sees me as more of the sidekick in a buddy movie.

I guess I need a new best friend anyway, so . . . lucky me.

To Be Continued . . .

END SCENE.

DUFFY

Thursday

Feeling = Brains should be able to throw up like bodies.

Then I could flush my memory of Rosco's down the bowl and be done with it. But no. I just get to feel sick for the rest of my life because I needed the Orphan to rescue me.

Feeling = UGH! Thinking about it literally makes me say that. Out loud.

UGH!

The whole double date thing felt a little slick to begin with but Sheridan is chill so I figured Audri would be too. She's not. The girl must sink a lot of ships because she's all loose lips. First she was filibustering about *X Factor* like this new season is going to help us win the war on terrorism. Jagger and I are just sitting there like two dudes tied to a radio that won't turn off. He probably doesn't even know what *X Factor* is. I'm not exactly a fan either but Mandy and Bubbie Libby are, and Demi Lovato is kind of hot so I tolerate it. But that's the last thing a guy wants to admit while his teammates are killing themselves laughing because the hostess announced that he's wearing cologne.

UGH!

I know Jagger can't take it either because at one point he leaves to go to the bathroom. So now I'm tied to the radio alone and getting texts from the guys complimenting me on my "perfume," and I want out. I'm about to tell Sheridan my mom needs help with something so I can leave but the food comes. Then I'm glad I stayed because Sheridan is eating in a way that Mandy, Morgan, and Megan never would and it makes me happy. Not that she's some turkey I'm trying to plump up for Thanksgiving. I just think it's cool that she doesn't have to talk about stuff that doesn't matter and I wanted to tell her that, because Bubbie Libby said girls like boys who appreciate girls.

Feeling = Or something like that.

Anyway, I told her that eating meant she had passion. I'm not exactly sure how that adds up but Amelia always says it and it made Sheridan smile so I felt pretty good about things. Then I felt awful again because Audri and her loose lips were back on the scene. Only this time instead of filibustering my ears, she was filibustering Jagger's face.

It's not like I've never thought about kissing Sheridan because I have, but I wasn't about to do it in a public pie shop, especially with all my ex-friends watching. But she was obviously hurt because she wouldn't look at me and when Mandy doesn't look at Gardner it means he did something wrong.

UGH!

So I'm trying to think of what to do but of course all I come up with is—run!

That's when I felt it. Jagger's knee knocking my knee. Like he was trying to tell me something. So I look down all sneakily, as if he's trying to pass a note in class. Then he takes something out of his pocket and jams it down the back of the booth. I slip it into my hand. It's a plastic ball with a ring inside.

Feeling = Jagger is smooth.

Living on the streets must have sharpened his senses because the guy knew I needed to make things right with Sheridan and he helped me out. Not like a buddy, like a brother. Or Yoda.

I waited until we were walking home.

ME: Things were kind of weird in there.

SHERIDAN: Tell me about it.

ME: I know.

(We watch a car drive through a puddle like it matters.)

ME: Anyway, I want you to know, you know, where I'm coming from and...

SHERIDAN: And what?

ME: And that kind of thing.

SHERIDAN: O-kay...

128

ME: So, here.

I give her the plastic ball. She opens it. I kind of laugh because I didn't realize the ring said *Best Friend*.

Feeling = Like a bit of a One Direction dude telling a girl I'm into her and that she's my best friend at the same time. But I guess she is my best friend because she's my only friend so...

SHERIDAN: Wow.

Feeling = She was so speechless she barely talked the rest of the way home.

Feeling = I owe Jagger big-time.

−LATER

Lily

Friday, October 26, 2012

No, John Lennon, you're not the only one. I too imagined all the people living life in peace. At least for today, the day I, Lily Bader-Huffman, turn fifteen. But alack, I'm a dreamer too.

Do you know how agonizing it's been watching Blake delete me from his life and replace me with Vanessa? What am I saying? Of course you do. You had your share of drama with the Beatles but *you* broke up with *them*. Don't worry, John, I'm not going to take the easy route and blame Yoko because Mom has brainwashed me against speculative gossip. But I will say this: You know why the band broke up. You know what the fighting was about. You died knowing. Lucky you.

Me? I've been in a cold war for ten days, frozen out by my enemies for no apparent reason. I've been desperate to wave the white flag and offer my pride in exchange for answers. Instead, I held firm, pretending I was too busy to care. When really I was certain that whatever I did to get Blake's slim-fit indigo J.Crew denims in a bunch would be forgiven on the anniversary of my life. Or at the very least, explained in a heartfelt card. So I held my tongue, blinked back my tears, and hoped that if I could just make it to today...

By last period Blake still hadn't wished me happy birthday and I panicked. It was the only special day I'd have for another year. If not now, when? The window of forgiveness was starting to close. If I didn't force it open I'd be left outside forever.

I followed Blake to English and begged him to talk to me. He refused so I followed him into class. Then I sat on his desk. He told me to go away in that angry whisper of his. I angry-whispered back, "Never." I didn't care if Ms. Silver sent me to the principal's office. I didn't care about anything but peace and I was ready to fight for it.

Blake realized this once Ms. Silver started teaching and I was still there. He nudged the small of my back. *Go.*

I readjusted my posture. *No.*

Ms. Silver tilted her head like a confused dog. She glared at me. I glared back.

"Can I help you, Lily?" she asked.

"No, thank you," I said. "But Blake can. Is it okay if I talk to him in private for a minute? It's urgent."

A few guys made that stupid *ooooh* sound like Blake was about to get some. Others laughed. Ms. Silver rolled her eyes at their immaturity and said, "Ahhhh, the lost art of communication...a perfect segue to today's discussion on *Cyrano de Bergerac*." She waved us toward the door like that cool usher at the Independent who helped us sneak into the Fellini festival.

Once we were in the hall I began to cry. I couldn't help it. It was the first time I had seen Blake's eyes in almost two weeks and they seemed dead and hard in a way they'd never been before.

"Has Vanessa turned you into a zombie?" I asked, wiping my cheeks.

"*That's* what you had to ask me?"

"No. But it's the only thing that makes sense."

He put his hands on his hips and sighed like we'd been through this a thousand times.

"Seriously, Blake, I have no idea what this is about. Are you mad because I was gone for six days? Because that wasn't my fault and you know it."

He stared blankly down the hall.

"So that's it? I get pulled out of school and cease to exist. Replaced by some girl you didn't even want to hang out with last week? Better get a harness and some carabiners for all that social climbing."

Blake began wheezing. "Yeah, Lily. This is about social climbing."

"Then what?" The tears came back. "Tell me, because so far zombie is my only lead."

"Try outed by my best friend and I'd say you were on to something."

Outed?

"Stop trying to act, Lily. Your attempt at shock makes you look constipated."

"Act? I'm not trying to act. I have no idea what you're talking about."

"Really. Then why did Mandy Duffy come up to me last week and ask for a 'gay guy's take' on her mullet skirt?"

"*What?* She asked you that?"

Blake took a hit off his asthma inhaler. "Yeah."

"What did you say?"

"I said, 'If you want a gay guy's take on your mullet skirt, ask a gay guy.' Then I bolted. I've been avoiding her ever since."

"I know how she feels," I mumbled.

"I'm not avoiding you, Lily, I'm divorcing you."

"But—"

"You told Duffy, didn't you?"

My lungs tightened.

"I had to. He asked if we were a couple. I wanted him to know we weren't so he'd ask me out."

Blake took a quick hit off his inhaler "And how'd that work for you?" He hurried back into class before I could answer.

I stood there dumbfounded for the next five minutes. How would I survive Pub without Blake? How would I survive anything without Blake? Had I really betrayed his trust for a date with a non-Jewish guy who ignored the birthday banner I taped to my front door? Who gave an ironic *Best Friend* love ring to Sheridan Spencer last night? Yes. Yes I had. And I hated myself for it.

I slumped to the cold checkerboard tiles and sobbed into my knees.

A pregnant woman appeared above me and offered me her swollen hand.

"Come," she said. "We can talk about it in my office."

I had no idea who she was or if this "office" was even in New Jersey, but she hugged me when I stood so I said yes.

My pregnant angel was Mrs. Martin, the student adviser. A compassionate woman who eventually agreed to hook me up with a backbreaking work schedule. One that would leave no time to miss the friends I no longer had. The goal being I skip a grade or two so I can graduate early and go to college, where I belong. All I have to do is check in with her every week to prove I'm not losing my mind or peeing Red Bull.

I thanked Mrs. Martin for making me feel so much better. But the moment I left her office I felt horrible again, because guess who was sitting in the waiting room? Vanessa!

I was so shocked I accidentally said, "Hey." She didn't say a word back.

Now I'm in the library, where I will spend the next eight months of my life gathering dust with everything else in here that's not digital. Jagger is here too.

He's returning a book on exotic animals. He reminds me of

a lizard. Always looking around nervously. He had the right idea. Only instead of emancipating from my parents I'd cut ties with my birthday. Then today would have felt like a regular disaster instead of unassailable proof why I, Lily Bader-Huffman, never should have been born.

Lily Bader-Huffman-Duffy

DUFFY

Friday

Brandy the hostess must have told her boyfriend about WhispHer for Him because some dude named Daniel Ponnowitz just wasted $38.85 on three bottles.

Feeling = $2,035.15 to go before I'm out of the red.

—LATER

VARSITY VARSITY
VARSITY VARSITY
VARSITY VARSITY
VARSITY VARSITY
VARSITY
VARSITY VARSITY
VARSITY
VARSITY

Vanessa

October 26th

I've always been hard-core Mach[74] about Beni's. I didn't care how or why my family got there, as long as we did.

Ver? That's the lie I told myself.

It turns out I do care how and why we get there. I care a shedload. So much so, that I should be marched into the town square, stripped of my Mach-status, and have the video go viral.[75] You see, Journal, we went to Beni's last night. Mom and Dad didn't argue once. And I still had a Richter breakdown in the bathroom. Why? Because we weren't there to celebrate me.

....

[74] Machiavellian: The end justifies the means.

[75] I assume the event would be recorded.

It was all about A.J. getting his job back at Spencer BMW. Nary a single toast was made to the girl who cracked the case[76] or the one who forced Sheridan to set the record straight[77] or the one who persuaded A.J. to get over his anger and accept Mr. Spencer's generous offer.[78] Nary a one. And I'm not okay with that.

I started rattling off some of my B-list accomplishments so I could inject some sweetness into this very bitter dish.[79] Praise from a teacher with tenure...Acing the endangered animals quiz on the Girl Scout website...Washing the recyclables... Anything to resuscitate my dying status as an overachiever. I even considered announcing my romantic victory but it's not official until we Blake-out, and undeserved praise would have left me feeling emptier than no praise at all. I needed something real to keep me from suspecting what my roiling stomach already knew. That my eight-year reign as Queen Outstanding was over. But I had nothing. My Instagram likes are down by 6 percent, my Facebook comments are scant, my SWAP bracelets are still being held by U.S. Customs, I haven't received a single compliment since Blake asked where my green shirt ends and my eyes begin, my motivational tweets are not being retweeted, and my grades are all F's.[80] I have fallen off

---

[76] Me.

[77] Me again.

[78] Yep, all me.

[79] Not a bad phrase, considering my mood.

[80] F for Fake.

the Google Map and landed next to a pile of washed-up reality stars, injured athletes, and recalled dog food.

I was no better than the other customers at Benihana, including my brother. The more I realized this, the more I panicked. Had I peaked in middle school? Was it all downhill from here? Does A.J. have what it takes to keep my parents from divorcing? I hurried for the bathroom to experience what was later diagnosed as anxiety disorder.[81] Shortness of breath, distorted vision, eyes darting like a trapped animal. I am allergic to average.

Running circles around the competition will no longer suffice. I have to grease my proverbial wings and break the sound barrier. Raise Coach Speedman's 10 percent rule to 20 before this panic disorder allergy kills me.

So here I sit. Outside Mrs. Martin's office, with a list of queries including but not limited to "How do I win the Principal's Award?" "How can I become a member of the 2012–2013 Phoenix Five," and "How can I boost my likability on social media?"

I also have a list of un-askable queries including but not limited to "Why hasn't Blake tried to kiss me?" "When your parents stop sleeping in the same room is divorce inevitable?" "How can I get straight A's without cheating?" and—

FOE-M-G, Lily just walked out of Mrs. Martin's office.

I knew I should have wished her a happy birthday! I didn't have to mean it. I just had to say it. It wouldn't have made up

[81] Source: WebMD.com.

for stealing Blake but it might have kept her from telling on me. If that's what she was doing. Which it had to be. She smirked right at me!

Stay calm, Vanessa. Don't panic. Don't look at her. Keep writing. Write. Write. Write. This isn't getting graded. It doesn't have to be good. Just write, girl. Write!

I should have killed her with kindness. Offered to take her out for a birthday ice cream. Treated her to a triple scoop and then apologized for unfriending her. I could have convinced her to drop the hacking thing. I could have done something. But I didn't. I'm just sitting here, breath shortening, vision distorting, eyes darting.

Now I am fanning my pallid complexion with a brochure on taking a stand against peer pressure. I need to leave. I can't face Mrs. Martin now. She knows…so itchy…losing saliva… must keep writing…It's keeping me from fainting…My EpiPen is a peppy pen…Talk me down, PeppyPen…Keep me grounded…No, don't. I have to stand. I have to get out of here. Too late. Here comes Mrs. Mar—

Lily

Date: Still my birthday

I closed my eyes, wished for Blake to forgive me, and blew out the candles. Mom cut the carrot cake while I tried to smile. My present, a white envelope propped up against a half-empty ketchup bottle, looked about as promising as my future.

"Any plans tonight?" Dad asked.

"Nope."

"Where's Blake?"

"Sick."

"What about the others?"

He was referring to the Homies. Even he knew I didn't have friends at Noble.

"They offered but I have a paper to write," I said. "Which reminds me, where can I find 1972?"

"Excuse me?" Mom said, licking icing off her thumb.

"I need more typewriter ribbon."

Dad almost choked. "You're not using *that* old thing, are you?"

I nodded.

"Typed my first article on it," he said. "A headless body was found at a topless bar."

"It still works?" Mom asked.

"No. Poor guy bled to death."

Mom giggled as she handed Dad some cake.

"Why don't you use your computer?" he asked.

"A typewriter is faster."

As expected, that led to a series of inquiries about my bat mitzvah savings account and why I wasn't allocating those funds toward a laptop.

"I spent it on a back-to-school wardrobe."

Mom gasped. "Not those androgynous European club kid clothes."

I nodded.

"You paid for those?"

"Someone had to."

My parents exchanged a conspiratorial look.

"As much as you detest conformity, there are certain inalienable rights that come with being part of the public school system," I said. "The right to modern clothing, the right to technology—including but not limited to high-speed Internet—and the right to choose my own luncheon meats. If you don't want to grant me these rights, fine. Homeschool me. But if you want me to survive the persecution of public—"

"What is it you need, Lily?" Mom asked.

I looked at her with an inappropriate amount of sass, but really? She needed me to spell it out for her?

"A computer, Mom. Clothes. Normal sandwiches. A fighting chance!"

She handed me the envelope.

I turned it around in my hand, politely intrigued.

"Go on," Dad said. "Open it."

I did. There was a white gift card inside. The logo—an apple with a bite taken out of it—looked wonderfully familiar. I assumed it was a biblical reference to Eve's sin in the Garden of Eden. "What is this?"

"As you would say, a first-class ticket to the year 2012," Mom joked.

"The Apple store?"

"I'm tired of sharing my typewriter," Dad said. "Go get a computer already, will ya?"

I screamed for joy.

We laughed and hugged and ate cake.

Before going upstairs I thanked them for everything, including but not limited to loving me for fifteen straight years in a row.

Lily Bader-Huffman-Duffy

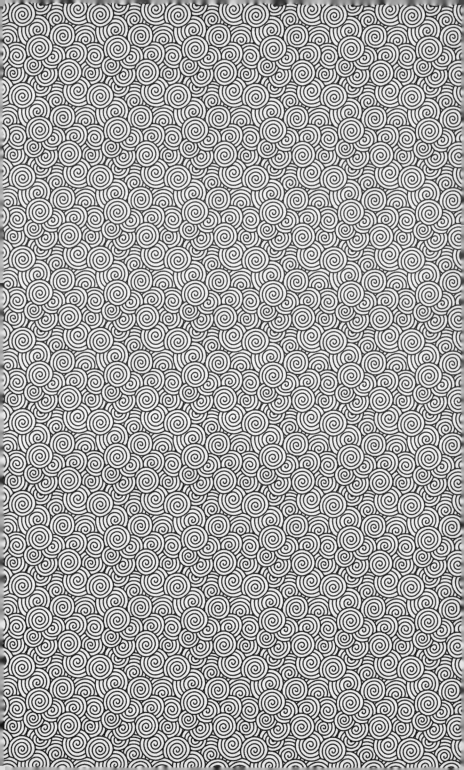

Sheridan

10.26.12

INT. NOBLE HIGH GYM—HOME TEAM BLEACHERS—NIGHT.

DUFFY bounces the ball toward the net. Excitement builds. SHERIDAN's pear-shaped bottom hangs off the lip of the bleacher in anticipation. DUFFY lifts the orange orb. He aims, he shoots, it soars, he scores! SHERIDAN jumps to her wedges and cheers for DUFFY. RANDOM GIRLS cheer for him too. Some wave signs. Others claim they love him.

My clenched fist says they better not mean that.

Channeling Khloe Kardashian with a black beanie, gold hoop earrings, skinny jeans, and a stylishly baggy black tee,

I looked every bit the part of a baller's girlfriend. Except for the ring, which I turned around the moment the Encryption waved goodbye and went into the locker room. Yes, I call Duffy *the Encryption* because he is sending me some serious mixed messages.

O'course I don't say this to his face. The only noun I would ever share that with (besides "journal") is Audri because we live for nicknames. But Audri went to Octavia's so I haven't told her yet.

Why do I sound so un-jealous of Audri's Friday night sleepover?

Glad you asked.

FLASHBACK.

Audri and I walked to school together today—alone—for like the first time in a dog's ear. I told her that and she cracked up because apparently the expression is "dog year." I think she's wrong about that but I didn't tell her. We were having a much needed moment and I didn't want to knock the boat.

Actually, at first I did want to knock the boat. I wanted to knock it hard so she would fall off the edge and land in shark-infested waters because she made me feel so seriously awk at Rosco's. I even pretty much told her that.

So, was it embarrassing? (Me.)

Was what embarrassing?

Making out in public like that? (Me.)

No. It was a total turn-on. (Audri.)

I stopped walking.

What? (Audri, confused.)

Sorry. My internal organs seized. I'll be okay in about an hour.

Seriously, Sher? (She grabbed my wrist and began pulling me down the block. I resisted. She let go. Her celery-stick body was no match for the pear.) *If you act like a prude every time I tell you something like this I'm not going to be honest with you anymore.*

I'm not a prude, Audri. I just know you and you're not like this.

Like what?

All . . . (I wiggled my Rubenesque hips and made a show of feeling myself up.)

How do you know what I am? (Audri.)

Really?

You know who I was, but I've changed. (Audri.)

Oh, you've definitely changed. And you know what? I'm fine with it. I'm happy you're making new friends, and that you have a sugar glider, and the lead in Wicked. *So stop acting like an archetype and get real.*

I'm not acting like an archetype.

Are too.

Are not.

Are. End scene.

Puh-lease. Audri cleaned her glasses with her seriously tight Michael Stars tee, glared at me through clear lenses, and asked, *Which archetype?* Like that was even my point.

The masquerader? The thrill seeker? The child?

Audri's jaw hung slack. *Don't hold back.*

Okay, the betrayer, the seducer, the—

The seducer?

Too far?

I know.

We laughed.

I have been known to take a soapbox and run with it but I was on to something and we both knew it.

We walked the next block in silence. Then out of nowhere, that *Skippyjon Jones* book Mom reads to the twins popped into my head. It's about a Chihuahua who pretends he's a cat. And for some reason that summed up how I was feeling. Audri is a PG-13 who's pretending to be an R.

Admit it, Sher. You're still mad because I've branched out.

More like sold out. (Me with a perfect comeback.)

You sound like my therapist. (Audri.)

Roslyn?

No, Susan.

(Yay. Susan is the one she likes so I continued.)

Audri, you can have friends without acting slutty, you know. Because that's not who you are and that's not what Jagger likes about you. Same with Octavia, only with her you're being all Florence Nightingale even though you know she's faking and sick people make you dizzy.

Okay, I get it, you're not jealous. (Audri, annoyed at my soapboxing.) *You want me to be me.*

Exactly.

So if I tell you I'm sleeping at Octavia's tonight, you won't be mad?

I'll only be mad if you leave Mr. Cozy at home.

But—

Audri, I've tolerated that nubby Honey Nut Cheerios–scented blankie for nine years. If Octavia is a real friend she'll put up with it too.

She thought about it for a second and then said, *I hear ya.*

We were running to first period when I remembered that I forgot to tell Audri about my humiliating Best Friend ring. Maybe it was for the best (pun intented). I was obviously channeling someone levelheaded and mature—like Hailee Steinfeld or Ivanka Trump—and decided it would benefit our relationship if I stayed in that headspace awhile longer. At least until sundown. So while Audri and Mr. Cozy went to Octavia's, I went to the Flames/West Orange game dressed as a baller's boo.

END OF FLASHBACK.

CUT TO:

DUFFY scores another basket. SHERIDAN stands and cheers.

If I knew I'd be doing all these squats I would have worn m' Hard Tails. (Me to the girl beside me.)

Ha! (Her, saying "ha" instead of laughing it.) *That Duffy is the real deal.* This black-haired chipmunk-cheeked sophomore's name was Ivy.

I know all about Duffy. He's the reason I'm here. (Me as Khloe.)

You and every other girl. You know, except me. I've been hanging with #7 for three weeks.

Ha! (Me, saying "ha" instead of laughing it.) *Ivy has been hanging. Get it?*

At least once a day.

Ha.

I wasn't sure which "it" she was referring to so I was relieved when the Encryption scored and we could move on.

While THE CROWD cheers, some older HUSSY (junior) runs onto the court, grabs DUFFY's face, and kisses him, mouth closed but on the lips. She runs back to her seat all proud and leaves him standing there all stunned. Other HUSSIES hiss like the FIRST HUSSY stole their man. One even screams, "I want your wrist cuffs!"

SHERIDAN's bright expression is eclipsed by a dark thought. She sits. THE CAMERA ZOOMS IN as denim-encased legs surround her like prison bars. She doesn't feel like a leading lady or even a best friend. More like an extra in a straight-to-DVD movie about a high school basketball hottie who got too big for life in a small town.

You okay? (Ivy sits down too.) *I didn't shatter your dreams or anything, did I?*

O'course not. (Me, trying not to sound shattered while also trying not to look like someone who just found out her crush is a potential player.) *Duffy invited me here. We've been hanging for a few weeks too.* (I thumbed my ring to make sure *Best Friend* was still facing my palm.) *Anyway, he's not my dream. Acting is.*

I knew I liked you. (Ivy.)

You act?

Every chance I get. I'm saving for Coachella.

They pay you?

Handsomely.

Commercials, right? (Me, trying not to seem superlatively impressed.)

Movies.

Impressed shape-shifted to depressed. Ivy was friendly and attractive but she didn't have "it." So why her? Why her and not me?

Which movies?

Let's see ... Last year I did Gimme Shelter, Drama Class, Bad Parents, Turnabout, Now, Forager, Leaving Circadia, *and* The Grand Theft. *This year—*

What? How?

Extra work, baby. Free food, a paycheck, and celebrity sightings. It's the bomb dot com.

Ah. (Me. Relieved.) *Do you meet casting agents?*

All the time.

Directors?

Yep.

Two buzzers went off—one from the scoreboard and the other in my brain. Duffy's game was over, mine was beginning.

Can you get me in?

Everyone hurried to congratulate the Flames. Ivy checked her phone. *I'm booked on* Jersey Shore *tomorrow night. You want in?*

Yes! (Me, bobble-heading.)

Done.

I hugged Ivy so hard she coughed. *Let's go say hi to the guys.* (Her, trying to escape my appreciation.)

I agreed because Ivy had just offered me my first professional gig and I didn't want to take off on her. Not because I wanted to stand like a bodyguard behind the Encryption while he humbly thanked a mass of hussies for projectile-puking compliments all over him. Not because of that at all. Just so you know.

To Be Continued...

END SCENE.

Duffy

Friday

I reread the stuff Officer Boyle said to me. Turns out the guy is a prophet.

You're a good-looking boy, Andrew, and you're at that age. Girls are going to do some wild things to get your attention. Get used to it, son. Heck, enjoy it. There are worse problems, kid.

Not that I'm the kind of guy who wants to reread compliments from cops. But last night was the kind of night that'll make a guy wonder if the Force is with him.

Feeling = The Force from *Star Wars*, not the police force. But thinking of the one from *Star Wars* made me think of the police one, which made me think of Officer Boyle, which made me look back to 10.12.12, which made me realize that there is no Force, I'm just good-looking.

I'm not trying to sound like Mandy, who acts all surprised when Megan or Morgan tells her some dude thinks she's hot. She's all: Seriously? Why would he even say that? You're so much hotter than me . . . Filibust . . . Filibust . . . Filibust . . .

It's just that I'm not like Bieber or anything. Not that I think Bieber is hot. All I'm saying is that girls were into me last night like I was all "swaggy."

Feeling = 1) **Weird at first.**

I scored a lot in middle school but never had girls scream, "I love you." I guess high school girls are different.

2) Then it made me feel slick.

I didn't want Sheridan to think I was into the Screamers. Not that we're official or anything but I did give her a ring.

3) Then I felt guilty.

Because the Screamers made me feel like an NBA pro and I liked it.

4) Then I felt like a slick NBA pro.

After the game Sheridan asked if I wanted to walk home together. I did so I said yes. Then Hud and Coops said some guys were going to Bedrick's house. As in, Duffy do you want to come with us to Bedrick's house? It was the first time they asked me to do anything (other than die) since 10.8.12 and I really really want my friends back. I also heard Bedrick has an epic game room . . . so I said yes.

5) Then I felt like a slick NBA pro who was also a player.

Only instead of ditching Sheridan for another girl, I was ditching her for my guys, so it didn't seem as bad.

6) Then I felt better.

Because Sheridan said her dad could pick her up so it was no big deal. She is seriously the coolest girl who is also pretty.

7) Then I felt lucky because a girl like that likes me.

So I asked her if she wanted to get ice cream this weekend. She said no because she got booked for a TV show. I was about to ask her which show when I noticed her Best Friend ring was turned around.

8) Then I felt like she wasn't into me anymore.

That's when I realized she wanted to walk so we could have "the talk." Only I was in a decent mood for the first time in weeks and I wanted to stay that way as long as I could. Also the guys were right there. So I pretended I didn't know she wanted to have "the talk" and said, "Text later?" like everything was fine. Then I left.

9) Then I felt bad.

10) Then I felt like Bieber again, only cool.

I was all pumped to hang in Bedrick's basement and play air hockey but all the guys wanted to do was talk about the Screamers. So we played press conference instead.

THEM: Who were those girls?

ME: I dunno.

THEM: Why were they so into you?

ME: Dunno.

THEM: Maybe it's his cologne.

(Annoying laughs.)

THEM: Or those Wonder Woman cuffs he's wearing.

(More annoying laughs.)

HUD: Seriously, dewd, what are those?

ME: Heavy Metal Bands. The name is kind of Velveeta but they balance my arms so I can throw better.

THEM: Aren't they kind of heavy?

THEM: And metal?

COOPS: And band-ish?

(This time I laughed too.)

ME: They have that moisture-wicking stuff on the inside so they feel pretty good. I dunno. They were only $19.25. . . . Anyway, I scored eighteen points tonight so I guess they worked.

THEM: Where'd you get 'em?

ME: Online.

I pulled up the Trendemic site on my phone and showed them.

Feeling = Slicker than the Situation's hair.

THEM: One of your stalkers said she liked them.

ME: Don't say that word.

THEM: What?

ME: Stalker. I have one. It sucks. She stole my lucky sneaks.

THEM: You have a stalker? For real?

ME: Yeah.

THEM: Sheridan?

ME: No. She's super cool.

THEM: You into her?

ME: We hang.

They looked all impressed.

THEM: So who's the stalker?

ME: Lily Bader-Huffman.

COOPS: She's kinda hot.

ME: All yours, guy.

COOPS: Thanks.

HUD: Hope she's into Darth Vader boots.

COOPS: I got this boot protecting you, Princess, so watch it.

THEM: How did you get to be such a player?

ME: It's the bands. I think they really work.

THEM: No. The other kind of player.

HUD: Yeah. Girls weren't that into you in middle school.

ME: I dunno.

Feeling = I really didn't. But the guys were talking to me again so I went with it.

ME: I guess the high school ladies know a good thing when they see one. Hey, let's see if these bands work for air hockey. . . .

They did. I won seven games in a row.

—LATER

Saturday

I woke up to a call from Anton. Last night I sold nine sets of Heavy Metal Bands and sixteen bottles of WhispHer for Him.

Feeling = $2,035.15 - $380.45 = $1,654.70!!!

Feeling = Take out the "l" in "player" and you have "payer." I'm both.

— LATER

Sunday

There's a shoelace missing from one of my hiking boots.

I told Mom they wouldn't be safe outside. She didn't believe me. She said only a crazy person would want those muddy old hiking boots.

Feeling = She was right about that.

— LATER

Sheridan

10.27.12

INT. BEDROOM—CLOTHES CLOSET—DAY.

SHERIDAN searches for an appropriate costume for her first paying gig. Overcome with emo-
tion and overwhelmed by options, she sits on the
closet floor, hugs her knees to her chest, and
lifts her gaze skyward. A cityscape of clothing
looms overhead. She feels like a tourist in Times
Square; small, timid, poorly dressed.

I seem to be channeling an animated mouse. Male, for some
reason. Dressed in a blue beret and red scarf. I'm all alone in
the big city cowering from heartless pedestrians.

CUT.

Where am I even going with this? I need to stay focused on my shoot tonight.

SHERIDAN lights some sage. She waves its cleansing smoke around her bedroom, hoping to rid herself of the negative energy brought on by ANDREW DUFFY.

I went to the game last night thinking he only wanted to be friends and I left *knowing* it. Does it sting like the bite of a thousand bees? Worse. But I must channel an Olympic pole vaulter and get over it. I have two scenes tonight, neither of which calls for an extra with emotional baggage.

To Be Continued...

END SCENE.

OMG, I have two scenes tonight!

To Be Continued...

END SCENE.

AHHHHHHHHHHHHHHHHH!

To Be Continued...

END SCENE FOR REAL THIS TIME.

Jagger

Oct. 27.

Mother asks if I like the lamb chops.
    LIE #37: Yes.

    Q: Then why aren't you eating them?
    A: (LIE #38) I will.

    I scrape off the green jelly when she's not looking.
    The chops still taste like toothpaste.
    Noodle doesn't care. That dog Dyson's up the minty meat
as fast as I can drop it.
    All done, I say. Then I stand.

Not yet, Father says.

I sit.

— Your mother and I have some bad news.

I hope he says they're going to jail so I can stop lying.

He doesn't. He says Governor Christie declared a state of emergency for New Jersey. Hurricane Sandy is expected to make landfall on Monday and we need to prepare for the worst.

I'm not sure what "the worst" means. I bite my fingernail anyway.

Father tells me not to worry. He will do everything he can to make sure the annual Legacy Hygienics Halloween Carn-Evil still happens.

Mother says if we have to move it inside, so be it.

I bite my thumbnail.

Father reminds me that nail-biting is a sign of weakness. It shows that you're nervous. That, and rapid blinking, will kill a negotiation.

— Okay.

I stand again.

— Not yet, Mother says. I'd like to know what is making you so nervous.

— I think I'm going to skip CarnEvil this year.

They look at me like I asked to be emancipated for real.

Q: Why? Father asks.

A: I made plans with a friend.

Q: What plans?
A: Neighborhood stuff.

Q: What kind of stuff?
A: Going to houses, I guess.

Q: You *guess*?
A: I always go to CarnEvil so I don't know *exactly*. Whatever normal people do on Halloween.

Q: And we're not *normal*?
A: (LIE #39) That's not what I'm saying.

(That's exactly what I'm saying.)

Q: What are you saying?
A: I want to do something else this year.

Q: Who is this *friend*?
Q: What's his name?
A: (LIE #40) Au——nette.

Q: His name is *Aunette*?
Q: Are his parents European?
A: Aunette is a girl.

Q: A *girl*?

Dad refills their wineglasses.

Q: Is Aunette your girlfriend?
A: I guess.

Q: You *guess*?
A: Yes. Yes, Aunette is my girlfriend.

It tingles when I say that because, other than the name, it's true.

Q: Why haven't you mentioned her before?
Q: Or introduced us?
Q: Or invited her to dinner?
Q: Or to a Legacy function?
A: (LIE #41) No reason.

(There are 41 reasons.)

Q: How about taking her to CarnEvil? We'll all ride together.
(You're in prison.)
A: (LIE #42) She doesn't like crowds.
(On death row.)
A: (LIE #43) She's claustrophobic.
(I live in a pet store.)

Father exhales sharply.
— The party is outside, he reminds me.

— Not if Hurricane Sandy hits, I remind him back.

Father looks at Mother like this is her fault.

— Daniel, honey. You love this party. You always have, Mother says.

— I know. But I want to hang out with my school friends this year.

(Because I have school friends this year.)

— Family first, Father says.

— Family's *always* first, I say.

— Most kids would appreciate what you have, Mother says.

(Like Jagger.)

— So give my ticket away.

Father takes the napkin off his lap and tosses it on his lamb scraps.

— Rosemary, I'll take my brandy in the den.

Then Mother says, any girl who tries to come between you and Legacy is bad news and not worthy of a Ponnowitz boy. Do you understand?

— Yes, Mother.

This time when I stand they let me leave.

I go to my room and write the whole thing down so I remember my lies. That's what I'm doing now.

The crazy thing? Audri doesn't come between me and Legacy. Legacy comes between me and Audri.

That won't change unless I tell her who I am.

First, I need to decide who I am.

Daniel or Jagger?

Technically, I am both.

166

Realistically, that won't fly.

Noodle is barfing outside my bedroom door.

Mother just arrived on the scene.

Daniel, why is your dog regurgitating lamb on the carpet?

LIE #44: No idea, Mother.

-J

Vanessa

October 27th

Mrs. Martin did not question my outstanding GPA or how I earned it. In fact, she fully supports my desire to make like Microsoft and Excel. She upgraded my classes to AP, constructively criticized my social media posts to make me more "likable,"[82] and shared the credentials of past Phoenix Five

---

[82] "Perhaps you should steer away from personal goals and Deepak Chopra quotes. Post details that your peers will find relatable. For example: favorite study snacks, news on a clothing sale, cute animal pics."

winners.[83] Thusly, I was certain that Lily hadn't told on me, so I was able to leave school yesterday with a scintilla[84] of hope.

#HurricaneSandy is trending right now because she is expected to hit land Monday. In an attempt to stay #relatable and #likable I just tweeted: *Will be singing in the rain. #HurricaneSandy*. With a link to the following playlist. (Get it? Singing in the rain?)

Self Hypnosis—Positive Affirmations for a Better Life—
    The Subliminal Mind
Green Eyes—Erykah Badu
Forget—Lianne La Havas
On & On—Erykah Badu
At Your Best—Aaliyah
Want U Back—Cher Lloyd
Breathe—Blu Cantrell feat. Sean Paul
Break My Stride—Blue Lagoon (radio edit)
Big Girls Don't Cry—Fergie
Wide Awake—Katy Perry
The A Team (by Ed Sheeran)—performed by Birdy
One Step at a Time—Jordin Sparks
Perfect—Pink

---

[83] Perfect grades, ABC soap opera star, teen ambassador for homeless women, winner of statewide poetry slam. I asked her what the fifth person did. She said she was still talking about the first. I said I had heard enough.
[84] I like this word.

I already got RT[85] nine times[86] and favored by thirty-six people.[87]

O my G, @BlakeMarcus just this second tweeted:

@Vanessacharlotriley Epic list #greatmindsthinkalike.

Mom and Dad are arguing downstairs about who dented the Nissan. Normally, I'd escape to the roof, but it's too windy. Not that it matters. I don't even itch! Theory: Mrs. Martin has provided me with the tools I need to regain my #1 status. The promise of a better tomorrow has cured my allergies.

I am a phoenix rising from the ashes! A butterfly emerging from a chrysalis! Teen Jesus![88]

Ver? Why put a label on it? For the first time in a long time there's hope. That's the real takeaway here.

---

[85] Ms. Silver, this means "retweeted." It's a Twitter thing.

[86] Once by Blake.

[87] Including Blake.

[88] I know. Too far.

Vanessa

October 28th

Mom found a plain white envelope under the welcome mat this morning. It was addressed to me. The note inside was typed with an old-fashioned typewriter.

THE TRUTH WILL BE REVEALED.

How Lily is that? I'm done.

Eyes darting. Can't breathe. These threats are weighing heavily on me. I can no longer carry them alone. I need A.J.

———

I'm back and breathing thanks to the empty bag of microwave popcorn I found under A.J.'s bed.[89] Yes, I told him everything. His first question was, "Think she's gonna tell on me too?"

"I don't think so."

He kept shuffling and reshuffling a deck of cards. It was working my last nerve. He said it helps him think.

"Lily doesn't want to turn you in."

"How do you know?" I asked while breathing into the bag.

"I have a lot of experience with threats," A.J. said. "She would have done it already."

"Then what's with the notes?"

"She wants an apology."

"For what?" I asked, even though I knew.[90]

A.J. stopped shuffling long enough to flash Dad's classic you-really-don't-know smirk: head cocked, brows raised.

"Fine."

I decided on a handwritten apology because Ms. Silver says emails siphon the sentiment out of correspondences. So I will transcribe the following onto my VCR[91] embossed stationery and deliver it tomorrow at school.

....

[89] When people get anxiety attacks they over-breathe. This lowers the level of carbon dioxide in the blood and makes them feel worse. Breathing into a paper bag builds up the carbon dioxide in your body again, so you should immediately start feeling better.

[90] Not showing up at school that night to change her grades. Stealing Blake. Ignoring her at school. Not wishing her happy birthday.

[91] My initials.

Dear Lily,

Happy belated birthday. I wanted to extend my wishes when I saw you outside Mrs. Martin's office, but I was afraid of getting snubbed. You see, I have been fragile lately and wasn't sure I could take any more rejection. I am sorry for that.

I am also sorry for not doing that thing I promised to do the night of Octavia's party. It's just that when Blake ditched me to hang out with you I was severely depressed and feared my skills would be compromised as a result. If only Blake and I were as solid then as we are today. But alas…

That said, will you ever forgive me for "stealing him away"? I put quotes around that phrase because I imagine that's what it feels like. I assure you, Lily, I had no intention of taking your place. You said you didn't have feelings for him and I don't think you were lying to me. I think you were lying to yourself. Only now it's too late because Blake and I are sort of a thing. You probably know that, though, since everyone at school has been calling us Blanessa.

Is this why you look so sad? I'd like to help you or, at the very least, expose you to the teachings of Deepak Chopra. He has helped me swallow my pride so I can ask for forgiveness and I'm sure he can help you, too. I'm not doing this for any reason other than I really miss being your friend. Veritas.

Please forgive me.

Sincerely,

Vanessa Charlot Riley

I just proofed this twice. I'm going to transfer it onto my stationery and then spend the day listening to the rain, drinking caramel lattes, and getting ahead on my homework. I hope A.J. is right about this. I guess I'll find out tomorrow.

Lily

Monday, October 29, 2012

At first I didn't care how dangerous Sandy was going to be. I wanted to wrap my loving arms around this Frankenstorm and thank her for keeping me out of school.

Now I'm not so sure. The winds are 80 miles/hour. I can't even see into Duffy's bedroom window because the rain is so thick. They say it's going to get worse in the next few hours, which means I can't do that thing I swore I wouldn't do anymore but still want to, because I can't go outside. Also because I shouldn't. I did it yesterday morning and it made me feel pathetic for the rest of the day. It should be noted, though, that while doing it I get a rush. Something about sneaking up to the house and—

Power just went out.

Vanessa

October 29th

School is canceled because of Hurricane Sandy, thusly, I can't give my apology letter to Lily. I ha—

O my G! A tree branch just smacked my window.[92] I can't take this anymore. Forgive me, Ms. Silver, for I am about to sin by emailing said apology to Lily. I have no choice. I need to know that she forgives me. My nerves can't live like this.

I proofed the email. Ready to hit "send." 1 . . . 2 . . .

Power just went out!

---

[92] I thought it was Lily!

Sandy or Lily?[93]
Can't breathe.

---

[93] What if Lily cut the wires?

Sheridan

10.29.12

INT. SPENCER HOME—BASEMENT—SURVIVAL MODE—LATE AFTERNOON.

The house shakes. Electricity is out. The future is uncertain. SHERIDAN stuffs her mouth with chocolate caramel corn to avoid screaming, "I'm not ready to die!" MOM and DAD hover around the emergency radio. The TWINS slice the darkness with blue light sabers. SHERIDAN steadies her quaking hand by putting quill to paper.

Candlelight flickers against the pages of her journal. Like waves, it undulates and sways, reminding SHERIDAN that her longtime battle with motion sickness is far from over. Nauseated, she moves away from the flame and turns on her phone, then the flashlight app; 11 percent battery power remains. She must tell her story with haste.

It begins with a wide-eyed girl and a dream. Shoot. Battery at 10 percent.

FLASHBACK.

EXT. SEASIDE HEIGHTS—BOARDWALK—SATURDAY EVE-NING.

The Atlantic Ocean looks silver under the dark-ening clouds. Wind blows through the deserted carnival with ease. There aren't any crowds to nav-igate or whirling rides to change its course. The approaching storm has transformed this "Home for Family Fun since 1913" into a ghost town. SHERIDAN, driven by unwavering passion and the need for TV credits on her resume, will not be deterred.

Ivy led me straight to the table inside the registration tent marked EXTRAS. My name wasn't on the list, but attendance was low because of the weather so I was given a CAST sticker and told to make myself comfortable. My eyes pooled with tears.

Don't be bummed. (Ivy to me.) *I'm sure some dumb PA forgot to give the extras coordinator my message. But you're in now, so . . .*

Bummed? No, I'm excited. (Me.)

"Excited" was a superlative understatement. I felt like an alien who, after fifteen years of searching the universe, had finally come home. I wasn't channeling an alien, though. I was channeling Samantha Boscarino from the Nick show *How to Rock*. Not Molly, her character, and not her body because she's a carrot, not a pear. Really just Samantha's effortless style, which always seems to say, "Anyone up for a boardwalk stroll?" I was hoping that my knit cap and striped sweater would allow me to blend into the crowd, but at the same time poke out just a bit. Because that's the line an extra has to walk; a fine one indeed.

Personally, I thought I'd nailed it until Paige, the extras coordinator, said, "Lose the stripes. They stutter."

Really? They sounded fine in rehearsal. (Ivy. Joking, o'course.)

But I wasn't in the mood. All the T-shirt shops were closed and I didn't have options. I assumed my big break was broken until Ivy gave me a gray sweatshirt.

I declined. Politely, o'course. *Sorry, but I can't pull it off. Gray makes me look flu-ridden and sweatshirts box out my curves. I'd be fine with it if I was playing a character who wore unflattering clothes, but this is reality.*

So? (Paige.)

So, I'm supposed to be real. (Me.) *And I would really never wear gray.*

Paige laughed. *You think this show is real?*

I nodded yes. She fixed her eyes on mine, like fine print she was trying to read. *Oh honey, no. We have writers and wardrobe stylists and editors—all kinds of professionals who get paid to make this cast seem interesting. Reality is the nap they took this afternoon, before the cameras got here, and who wants to watch that?*

I must have looked like a kid who just found out that (SPOILER ALERT) Santa isn't real, because Ivy put her hand on my back and rubbed mom-circles.

So all this is . . . fake? (Me.)

No. Some of it's real. (Paige.)

Like what? (Me.)

Your hat. It's real cute. (Paige.)

Ha! (Ivy.)

Can I borrow it for Snooki? The clips on her extensions are showing and wardrobe took a weather day. It would really help.

I guess.

I sat, hoping to absorb this shock to my system. Not because I'm a fan of reality. I'm not. I can't stand reality—TV or otherwise. Hence the reason I want to not be me for a living. But to find out the entire genre is a lie? What next? Frosted Lucky Charms aren't magic? I needed to take five.

Ivy directed me toward the blue rectangle by the house. Now, color me a diva, but I refuse to cry in an outhouse for the same reason I won't puke in a toilet. It's superlatively gross and—

Uh-oh, battery at 8 percent.

Anyway, while searching for a sanitary place to cry, I happened upon a tent full of snacks. The tables were empty except for some *Vogue*-type woman with short hair, sipping tea. She was on the phone and didn't seem to notice me so I loaded a plate with mini cupcakes and cinnamon buns. I figured it was more professional to lick frosting than my wounds, at least on set. So I sat and ate and felt better instantly.

Hungry? (The woman.)

Her French accent made the question sound more like a judgment.

Been on set all day. I'm starving.

You usually heat that? (Her.)

Cupcakes? No, room temperature.

She shook her head no and then lifted an invisible fork to her mouth.

Oh, eat! (Me, cheeks burning.) *Um, not usually. Unless I'm trying to gain weight. Which I am . . . for a role.*

She lifted a perfectly plucked brow. *Impressive.*

Something about her chic hair and red lipstick made me want to keep impressing her. So I said, *I'm an experienced actress. This whole extra thing is just a favor, you know, for a friend.*

Do I know your work?

Maybe. Sheridan Spencer?

She shrugged. *I am Madelon Etienne.*

I asked what she did because I couldn't understand what a sophisticated woman like that was doing on a windy, deserted set like this.

I am a casting director.

My body tingled—toes to scalp.

Movies? TV? Theater?

Yes. And webisodes.

In New York?

Paris.

Oh.

This is my first job for America.

Oh! (I sat up taller and forgot that I was craving salt.) *What is it?*

A television show. Very huge in France. America just bought the rights.

What's it called?

Tut-tut-tut. (Madelon put a finger to her mouth.) *I cannot announce it yet. But I am looking for teenager types.*

Like me?

Perhaps. Stand up.

I did, and suddenly became aware of all my body parts at once, especially the pear-shaped ones. *I'm a small on top and a medium on the bottom, but I can easily change that.*

No. Your size is perfect. What is your age?

Twelve to nineteen.

Do you sing?

Mezzo-soprano.

Dance?

Ballet, modern, tap, jazz, river.

Madelon handed me a flyer. *Can you audition next Sunday?*

Yes! I was just about to hug her when a production assistant announced they were striking the set. The weather was getting worse. The shoot would be postponed until further notice.

Ivy felt terrible but I told her not to. It was the best job I never had.

END FLASHBACK.

INT. SPENCER HOME—BASEMENT—LATE AFTERNOON.

SHERIDAN's battery is about to flatline and she hasn't even written about THE ENCRYPTION yet. Not that she wants to waste her last 2 percent on someone who abandoned her on a basketball court Friday night and never apologized. She needs to weather this storm and then focus on her audition or she'll be all washed up. Pun intended.

To Be Continued...

END SCENE.

Jagger

Oct. 30.

I am watching CNN.

Eight million people don't have electricity.

If we didn't have a generator, that total would be eight million and three plus one dog named Noodle.

Sheridan

10.31.12

INT. SPENCER HOME—DAY THREE WITHOUT ELECTRICITY.

A blinding light wakes SHERIDAN from a deep sleep. She pulls the blankets over her head and screams, "I'm not ready!"

A familiar voice says, *Obviously.*

Oh, it's you. (Sheridan to familiar voice.)

Of course. Who'd you think it was?

Death.

Mom laughs. *Stop being so dramatic.*

Stop being so Mom-ish.

I've been calling your name for ten minutes. Are you ready?

I sat up and tried to focus but my eyes had nowhere to land. My room was end-of-the-world dark. The street outside my window was even darker.

We're ready to start the candy hunt. You should see your brothers. They look like real sumo wrestlers. She aimed her flashlight at my legs like a cop searching for something illegal. *Why aren't you dressed?*

Before Mom became a mom she was an off-Broadway costume designer. She says she doesn't miss it but I know she does, because every October she tweets things like, *Store-bought costumes are to Halloween what the plastic pine tree is to Christmas* and *RT this if you DIY on 10.31.*

She started stuffing and sewing H&M's girth suits in September and has been glue-gunning leaves and wildflowers to a flesh-toned unitard so I can channel Puck from *A Midsummer Night's Dream*. She's that passionate. Which is why she did not react well when I said I had decided not to dress up.

You can't just decide that!

I didn't. Governor Christie did when he canceled Halloween.

Sheridan, he said we have to stay indoors. He didn't say we can't have fun. She went on about how life doesn't always go the way we planned and how we have to adapt, not give up.

I avoided her eyes like I didn't agree even though o'course I did. I just knew I couldn't tell her that the unitard was too tight. She prided herself on taking accurate measurements. The news would be a dagger to her heart. I know how it feels to fail at the one thing you're passionate about. I'm an understudy, remember?

PAUSE FOR PRAYER.

Please let me nail my audition this Sunday. Please, oh please.

UNPAUSE.

Mom begged me to reconsider until I said the costume deserved a stronger debut. Something bigger than immediate family members and a dark house. This spoke to her and she left satisfied. Then I rolled over on a collage of bite-sized candy wrappers and went back to sleep.

To Be Continued...

END SCENE.

Lily

Saturday, November 3, 2012

Last Sunday morning, while I was supposed to be reading *Beowulf*, I found myself sneaking up to Duffy's to liberate his muddy hiking boots from the front porch. Then it started to rain and I figured he'd need them, so I took one of the laces instead.

At first I felt pathetic. I know that ferreting a boy's belongings is not a socially acceptable manifestation of desire. I'm not in-sane, after all—I'm in-fatuated; I know the difference. But my collection is about to dwindle because Mom is making me donate my "androgynous European club kid clothes" to the Hurricane Sandy relief drive today. And these items give me something to hold on to, something I can touch. Something other than hope.

Lily Bader-Huffman-Duffy

DUFFY

Saturday

The clothing and food drive was pretty decent. You know, for a clothing and food drive. But who's going to admit they're amped to be at school on a Saturday, even if it's for hurricane relief?

Feeling = Not me.

Still, girls hugged like they'd just come back from Iraq, and I bumped a lot of fists.

Feeling = Good. Bedrick's wasn't a dream. The guys liked me again for real.

I know that's a girly thing to say, but right when they started talking to me again, bam! I'm home for a week with

Sandy, Mandy, and no electricity. That'll mess with any guy's head. Not just mine.

Bubbie Libby made me donate her flowery housecoats. Hud and Coops wanted the Screamers to see me carrying grandma clothes, but the Screamers weren't around. Sheridan was. Boxing up cans of food.

She looked kind of messy and I like that. Not that she had crumbs on her lips or anything. That would be gross. Messy in a cool way. Like she was up for anything. Hair in one of those clumps on top of her head, old jeans, and a loose purple T-shirt. Maybe it was white. I forget.

I wanted to say hi but I didn't want to have "the talk" so I dumped Bubbie Libby's clothes on a table and turned away.

That's when I smashed into Lily and knocked everything out of her hands. Trendemic clothes were all over the wet grass.

Feeling = Whoa!

That's literally what I said. It was the opposite of I.D.E.A.L. (Ignore Don't Engage Avoid Leading her on). But I wasn't expecting to be that close to her face. I also wasn't expecting to see my shoelace tied around her wrist.

Hud cracked up, but Coops? He limped over in his Darth Vader boot—which his mom made him double-bag because of the flooding—and helped Lily pick her stuff up off the ground. He held up the paint-splattered jeans I sold her.

COOPS: You're getting rid of these? They're so cool.

LILY: All of it.

Feeling = Better. She obviously wasn't stalking me anymore.

Then I got a text from Sheridan. It said, *Busted. I know you saw me.*

Feeling = Life was easier when the power was out.

I turned to escape and there she was, walking toward me. I stood there and waved like some Derp who has no clue he's about to get "the talk." But I did know so I told Hud and Coops to gimme a minute because the only thing worse than "the talk" would be those guys making faces behind Sheridan's back while I got it. And I could tell by the way her arms were folded across her chest that I was about to get it good.

ME: Hey.

I was about to ask if she wanted to sit on the steps or something, but she laid into me before I had a chance.

HER: Don't flatter yourself. It's not like I'm obsessed or anything.

ME: Huh?

HER: I'm not one of your screaming fans so get over it.

Feeling = Harsh.

It was my turn to say something, I just didn't know what. So I put my hands in the pockets of my jeans, looked at my high-tops, and wondered what the guys in One Direction would say.

ME: I never said you were a screaming fan.

HER: Well, you act like you think I am.

ME: How?

HER: By constantly trying to remind me that we're "just friends."

ME: We are friends...right?

HER: Yes. So stop trying to remind me.

ME: Okay.

Feeling = Totally confused.

ME: Wait. How do I keep reminding you?

HER: Um, how about a ring that says *Best Friend*?

ME: Actually, I gave you that ring because I thought we were more than friends.

HER: Yeah, I know. *Best* friends.

ME: No. That's just what it said. It's not what I meant.

HER: It's not?

ME: No.

She looked at me like I was supposed to say more. I flipped up the mini blade on my Toolery ring ($24.99) and then shut it, because I didn't know what else to do.

ME: I mean, unless you want it to be like that.

HER: I don't.

ME: You don't?

HER: No. Do you?

ME: No. You?

HER: No.

We kind of stood there for a minute looking at the ground and the people walking by and the donation tables and the food trucks, everything but each other.

ME: Do you want to start wearing the ring again?

HER: Yes. But I kind of gave it to Audri.

ME: Audri? Why?

HER: She's my best friend.

ME: Ah.

Sheridan pointed at the chunk of silver on my finger. The one I was supposed to be advertising and selling so I could finally stop advertising and selling.

HER: I could wear that one.

ME: It's kind of big for you, don't you think?

HER: No.

ME: It's got all these blades and stuff in it.

HER: I know. I love that.

Feeling = What was I supposed to do?

I took off the Toolery and gave it to Sheridan. She said she'd wear it for luck on her audition tomorrow. Then she filibustered about that and everything else she did last week.

I wasn't yawning but I did go deaf while I thought about how much better things are, now that I have friends and a cool girl who wants to wear my ugly ring.

Feeling = I didn't want to leave but Mom made me. We need dog food.

— LATER

Jagger

Nov. 3.

I'm at Randy's Exotic Pets gearing up to order a sugar glider when Duffy comes in.

He asks where we keep the dog food.

Organic or regular, I say, like I'm working.

— I dunno, regular I guess.

— Second aisle on the left. If you see cat toys you've gone too far.

I know this because Noodle ate the regular before organic came out.

— You gonna hit the clothing drive at school?

LIE #45: I don't have anything to donate.

— Oh, that's right. Sorry, dude.

It's fine, I say.

But it's not. I don't want Duffy to think I'm the kind of guy who doesn't help out so I tell him about Wednesday.

— I can't believe you boxed hygiene products for eleven hours straight.

Funny how I'm finally telling the truth and he thinks I'm lying.

— How'd you get hooked up with such a big company? he asks.

LIE #46: Their top executive shares a cell with my pops.

— What's he in for?

— Dunno. It's not cool to ask.

Some guy in a safari shirt asks if we need help finding anything.

My heart starts pounding like a drum solo.

— I got this, bro, I say.

LIE #47: He's always stealing my customers.

— Derp, says Duffy.

— Yep.

Then Duffy thanks me for hooking him up.

LIE #48: It's my job.

— No, the other day. At Rosco's.

LIE #49: Oh. No big.

Only it *was* a big, 'cause I had no clue what he was talking about.

— Anyway, Audri has it now. Sheridan gave it to her.

LIE #50: Makes sense.

Then some girl walks by and tells Duffy he smells good. After she leaves he says he's not even wearing cologne today.

(I am.)

But I don't dare say that. I just want to get out of there before my cover is blown.

LIE #51: Randy needs me to run an errand. I better go.

I make it out of there and realize I never ordered the sugar glider. I also realize I'll never be the kind of guy random girls sniff.

Maybe that's not such a bad thing.

Sheridan

11.4.12

INT. HILTON HOTEL—BALLROOM C—ALMOST LUNCHTIME.

Rows of chairs rainbow across the ballroom as if facing a screen that isn't there. No matter. The jittery hopefuls who occupy them don't need to be entertained. They need to entertain. SHERIDAN SPENCER being chief among them.

She needs to stay centered, confident, connected to her creative epicenter. She needs to become her monologue ("I Dream" from *Little Shop of Horrors*) and inhabit her song ("Good Morning Baltimore" from *Hairspray*). She needs to adjust the black leotard that keeps riding up her butt.

They just called number seventy-seven. Two more, then me.

Usually these open calls are packed, but people are without power, and roads are flooded, and well, let's just say Mother Nature had my back on this one. Audri, however? Notsomuch.

FLASHBACK. ONE HOUR AGO. HILTON HOTEL PARKING LOT. SAYING GOODBYE TO MOM.

Make sure your phone is on. (Mom.)

I wasn't going to bring it. (Me.)

Why?

It's distracting.

Then I'm going with you.

But I need to focus. (And eat Skittles without being lectured on artificial dyes and processed sugar.)

Mom turned off the engine.

Fine, I'll bring it.

She turned it on. *I'll park right here. Call me if anyone looks sinister.*

I was tempted to show her the blade on the ring Duffy gave me, but that would make her worry even more.

I really like this ring. The weight of it. It's hard to write neatly with it on because it's so heavy, but I don't care. It connects me to Duffy in ways the plastic one could only dream of. Besides, that one didn't fit and I gave it to Audri. I saw it as a sign that Duffy and I were through, but my fingers were probably just bloated. Then, at the food and clothing drive, she dared me to get all Miss Piggy on his ass and confront him.

Not one to back down from a channel challenge, I did. Now everything with Duffy feels *yay*.

CUT.

GET BACK TO THE POINT.

I'm sitting in the first row of the rainbow to avoid sizing up the competition. It's my thing and it works. It's also my thing not to take calls or texts before an audition, but I hear Duffy's alert (popcorn) and I can't resist.

Break a leg. (His text.)

How *awwwww* is that? I snap a pic of me holding a bag of Skittles, ring showing. I'm about to write *Got me lucky charms* when a male voice shouts, *Number seventy-eight!*

So all I text is: *I'm next.*

I close my eyes and try to become Audrey from *Little Shop of Horrors*. Then my phone rings.

It's Audri.

Never, ever would I EVER pick up, but I was channeling Audrey when Audri called and if that's not a sign I don't know what is. So I tossed out the rule book and answered.

Did you go yet?

No, I'm next.

Break a leg! (Audri, sounding super supportive.)

Thanks.

Nervous?

Trying not to be.

Good. You're the best actress I know and ... What? ... Oh, hold on, Octavia wants to say hi.

Like a total idiot I said, *Okay.*

Hey, Sheridan. (Octavia.) *GOOD LUCK!*

My heart stopped. My scalp began to throb.

Why did you do that? (Audri in the background.)

Do what? (Octavia to Audri. I swear I could hear her smiling.)

You just cursed her! (Audri.)

Oopsie. (Octavia.)

FLASHBACK OVER.

I am trying to breathe. How could Audri have been so gullible? How could I? If only I had some sage or—

Number seventy-nine! (Male voice.)

Crap.

Seventy-nine?

I need to go.

Go, Sheridan. Go!

Seven! Nine! Seventy-nine.

Here. I'm here. (As in, here goes nothing.)

To Be Continued...

END SCENE.

Vanessa

November 4th

Intimacy should be genuine and heartfelt, never calculated. And certainly not motivated by insecurity, a need for validation or, dare I say, victory. But a Blake-out will promote me from "friend with chemistry" to "girlfriend" and I need that. I'll focus better in school if I know where I stand. Lily will be forced to accept her loss and my family will have another reason to celebrate. Everyone wins.

So I asked A.J. how one goes about making the first move.

"What are you, some kind of sex addict?"

"It's for a social studies paper. I need a guy's opinion, that's all."

"Are you asking what is *right* or what I *like*?"

"Aren't they the same thing?"

"Rarely."

"Fine, what is *right*?"

"Girls should never make the first move."

"Never?" This meant more waiting, and waiting is another thing that makes me itch.

"Once you're in a relationship it's fine, but never in the beginning," he said. "Or the guy will think it's okay to hook up, then bail."

"Why?"

"Because it wasn't his idea in the first place."

"That's so unfair!"

A.J. shrugged.

"How is that different from what you like?"

"I like when girls make the first move."

"Why?"

"So I can hook up, then bail."

"I hate you," I said, when what I really hated was how hard it is to be a girl.

One minute later, I texted Blake. He was at the mall and asked if I wanted to meet him there. I wrote back *yes*, double-brushed my teeth, and decided never to listen to A.J. again.

Then I emailed my apology letter to Lily. Could I have given it to her at school tomorrow? Perhaps. But I need closure as I am one hyperventilation away from dislodging my tonsils.

Now I wait....[94]

The less you open your heart to others, the more your heart suffers.

—Deepak Chopra

---

[94] It's been four minutes so far. Where is she?

Vanessa

November 4th

Blake spritzed some Abercrombie & Fitch cologne and then stepped into the mist.

"Any more Jagger-and-Audri sightings?" I asked, dropping make-out hints like breadcrumbs.

"We haven't been at school."

I scratched my arm. "Good point. But what do you think of their whole, you know, public display of A?"

He held up a black sweater and considered the brown elbow patches. "Too college professor?"

"I think it's kind of sweet."

Blake checked the price tag. "Not for a hundred and sixty-nine bucks."

"I mean PDA. Surrendering to the moment, not caring what other people think."

He bobbed his head to the blaring music.

"Blake!"

"Yeah?"

"Did you even hear what I said?" I was starting to sound like Grandma Lucy.[95] "Let's get out of here. These pictures of hungry models are starting to depress me."

"You're just as pretty as they are, you know."

All of me stopped. As in not just my legs, but my internal organs and brain function too. It was the nicest thing a boy of interest has ever said to me and I thanked him with a hug. He smelled like the store but I didn't pull away. I pressed closer.

"Now where?" he asked, detaching.

"Hey," a familiar-looking girl said to Blake. "You're in my brother's grade, right?"

"Yep," Blake said, kind of rudely.

"I'm Mandy. I asked you about my skirt that time."

Blake reached for my hand like he wanted her to know we were together, then he introduced me. I wanted to bounce up and down with delight but tried to appear unfazed, like holding my hand was something he always did.

"Nice to meet you, Mandy." I smiled like I wasn't the least bit threatened by her blondness or their skirt conversation. "You work here?"

....

[95] She gets cranky in loud restaurants.

"That obvious, huh?" she said, referring to her precisely cuffed skinny jeans, scrunched denim sleeves, and name tag. "It's dead today so I'm leaving early. Hashtag *Pretty Little Liars* marathon. How good is that show?" she asked Blake, not me.

"Never seen it."

"Yeah, right. Who's the little liar now?" Mandy said, with a wink and a wave goodbye.

Blake didn't wave back. Instead, he asked what I wanted to do next.

"We could go to J.Crew and say hi to Mike," I offered.

Ver? I wanted Mike's flirting to make Blake jealous. Maybe that would inspire him to make a move.

"He went home sick."

Ten minutes later I spotted Mike at the food court. He was ordering from Wok 'n' Roll.

Lily was standing beside him, wearing an ill-fitting man blazer.

My brain tried to process this shocking turn of events. I felt like the navigation system in Mom's car when she made a wrong turn.

Calculating new route . . . Calculating new route . . . Calculating new route . . .

Then suddenly, everything became clear. Lily and Mike are together. Blake feels betrayed and abandoned. He's been using me to make them jealous.

Blake Mach'ed me!

Were my feelings hurt? They are now. But at the time all I

216

could think was, *Our team has to win!* So I popped up onto my tippy-toes, clasped my arms around Blake's argyle scarf, and kissed him right there in the middle of the food court.

More like a Mach-out than a make-out, but I did it.

> *How to be adaptable: Take on more of the burden*
> *than you think you deserve.*

—Deepak Chopra

Lily

Sunday, November 4, 2012

Here's the crazy part. I, Lily Bader-Huffman, just returned from the mall with a 2012 MacBook Air, and that's *not* the lead story. This is:

I was passing J.Crew as Mike was walking out. He was wearing black-framed glasses that didn't have lenses. He was taking his lunch break and asked if I wanted to hang. I said no.

"Why not?"

"Um, because you don't like me. Because you won't give me your Friends and Family discount. Because you're probably happy that Blake stopped talking to me."

Mike whipped off his fake glasses. "Blake stopped talking to you?"

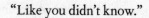

"Like you didn't know."

"I didn't. He stopped talking to me too."

"Sorry to hear that. Good luck with your life. Bye."

I had no intention of leaving without the full story, but I didn't want him to think he could shoot me the stink-eye for five months and get away with it. So I walked away.

"Wait!" Mike called. "My treat."

"I can't be bought," I said, wishing this exchange was with Duffy and not my ex-friend's ex-boyfriend, but I'll take the groveling where I can get it.

Mike put his glasses back on and started to cry.

Still, I didn't want to look like a pushover, so I said I'd have lunch with him if he gave me his blazer. You know, to make up for not sharing his discount. He gave it to me without hesitating and off we went to the food court.

It wasn't until we were in line, waiting to order egg rolls, that Mike started to talk.

"Blake dumped me," he said.

"Why?"

"He wanted a break."

"Maybe things were getting too serious," I tried.

"Not from me," Mike sniffled. "From gay."

"He wanted a break from being *gay*?"

"Yeah."

"Can you even do that?"

"*I* can't," he said.

The bald man in front of us turned around.

"*What*?" Mike snapped at him.

The man returned his gaze to the noodle displays glistening behind the glass.

"I can't just power down when it's convenient," Mike said. "This is who I am."

Unlike Blake, Mike didn't seem the least bit ashamed. I liked that.

"So what do you think it is?"

"I think he's met someone else. At Noble. And he doesn't want to tell me."

"I'd know if there was another guy," I said.

"Not a guy. That *girl*," he hissed. "That ... *Vanessa*."

"They're just friends."

"How do you know?"

"Because Blake is gay!"

Seeing Mike's tear-filled eyes through lens-less frames was too much to process. I had to look away. That's when I saw Blake and Vanessa. Kissing by TCBY.

"No way!" I blurted. Blake was using Vanessa to keep the rumors from spreading around school. And maybe he was pushing Mike and me away because he knew we'd call him out on it. Only instead of being angry, I wanted to curl into fetal and cry. Not just for Mike or Vanessa or Blake. But for anyone who has ever loved someone who couldn't love them back.

"What?" Mike asked.

I blocked his view and muttered something about the high cost of dumplings.

The sadness stayed with me all through lunch and even

while I was buying my laptop. Tragic, since that was supposed to be one of the happiest moments of my life. It was even with me as I began skateboarding home with my giant bag. Which is probably why I didn't really notice the rain, or the navy-blue Audi trailing beside me.

"Howdy, neighbor," the driver called over the blasting Taylor Swift song.

"Hi," I managed, before dropping my new laptop on the pavement.

"Is that highlighter on your nails?"

I nodded, my mouth too dry to speak.

"And a boy's blazer?"

I nodded again.

"Oh, girl, you need some serious help," she said. "Get in."

It was Mandy. I put my stuff in the backseat and jumped in. There was white dog hair on the upholstery, it smelled like Abercrombie perfume, and she kept slamming the brakes as she drove. Still, I felt like the luckiest girl in Jersey because I was in the same car that Duffy rides in; same seat!

She turned onto Foster Avenue and sighed. "This weather seriously bums me out."

"I hear ya," I said, wondering how a cooler person might have responded. Then I angled the heating vent away from my wet curls to keep them from frizzing, and searched for something small to take. A rolled-up piece of duct tape by my shoe was the best option.

"I just saw your friend," Mandy said. "The guy. The cute one."

"Blake?"

Saying his name felt like telling a lie.

"Yeah." She turned down the stereo. "What's his status, anyway?"

"Status?"

"Gay or straight?"

"Why?" I asked, suddenly irritated.

At the time I wasn't sure why her curiosity bothered me, but now I know. Like Blake, I didn't want it to matter.

"He's always hanging with that guy from J.Crew so I assumed they were a thing. But today it looked like he and Vanessa were into each other so . . ."

"So."

"Soooo, I hope I haven't been spreading the wrong information."

"What do you mean?"

"I want to be a professional gossip blogger, so credibility is a big deal. And if I've been telling everyone Blake's gay and he's not, then I need to post a retraction or something."

"Wait, why are you telling anyone anything?"

"He's hot, Lily. Girls want to know if he's OTM."

"OTM?"

She rolled her eyes like I should know. "On the Market."

"So *you're* why everyone knows?"

"Yes!" she said proudly.

"Not Duffy?"

"My *brother*?"

I nodded yes.

Mandy jammed the brakes and looked right at me. "Has he been taking the credit?"

The driver behind us honked his horn.

"No," I said. "I just assumed."

"No chance," Mandy said. "Duffy hates gossip. Same with our older sister, Amelia. They're freaks, I know."

"I could have sworn it was Duffy!" I said, relieved. "And that he wasn't talking to me because he felt guilty."

"No." Mandy turned to face me again. "He's not talking to you because you're a stalker."

I stiffened. "A *stalker?*"

I don't remember how she responded or if she even did. I do know that I managed to wiggle the ball of duct tape out of my shoe and return it to the floor mat without her noticing.

The moment she dropped me off I ran straight to Blake's house. Leaving my board, my new laptop, and my pride in Mandy's car.

Lily Baker-Huffman-Duffy

Jagger

Nov. 5.

Mother says my "new scent" is fighting with her squash blossoms and insists that I stop wearing it during meals.

Then Father says, it's about more than an off-putting smell, Rosemary. It's about loyalty to the family brand. Daniel should not be wearing a competitor's cologne.

I say, Legacy doesn't make cologne.

He says the Mini Mavericks can change that. Then he asks how the Mavs are doing lately.

LIE #52: Fine.

— I'd better not find out you've been skipping meetings for that... *girl*. What was her name?

I forget about LIE #40 and almost say Audri, but Mother saves me by accident.

— Aunette.

LIE #53: We broke up. You were right. She wasn't that into family.

This makes them happy. They forget about the cologne.

After dessert Father gets a text. He has to run to the office. Then Mother's masseuse comes by for a Rolfing. So I bike to Audri's because her mom is working late.

I'll be back before anyone notices I'm gone.

Sheridan is there when I show up.

She is lying on the couch under a blanket with a bag of Smartfood on her lap. Audri is opposite her under the same blanket.

I sit in the chair by the fireplace and smile like it doesn't suck.

They talk about some curse Octavia gave Sheridan. I wonder if that's what Duffy was talking about at the pet store so I ask if Sheridan passed it on to Audri.

This makes Sheridan angry.

— Is that what you're telling everyone? That *I* gave it to *you*?

— No!

— Because technically, *you* gave it to *me* by putting that witch on the phone.

— Sher, you're giving this curse too much power.

— Tell that to Duffy's silver ring. Oh, wait, it can't hear you because it slipped off my finger and landed at the bottom of a sewer.

Sheridan looks at her phone.

Stop chexting! Audri says. The audition was *yesterday*. Give them time.

Sheridan tosses her phone on the carpet and says, time for what? To pick someone who isn't cursed?

Then I finally get it. So I say, I get it! Because I do and I'm proud.

Audri goes, What do you mean you get it? How do you know about this stuff?

LIE #54: Guys know more than you think.

I'm not about to say my family makes T-words for "the curse," or that I heard it's contagious when girls hang out together. So I leave it at that.

But Sheridan and Audri go on and on about it.

I'm so bored my legs get restless. I change the subject before I kick in a wall.

— I saw Duffy at the pet store yesterday, I say.

Audri glares at me like I just blew up a sack full of kittens.

— *What?* What did I say?

She glares harder.

Sheridan asks if there was a swarm of girls around him.

Just one, I say. She liked his cologne. Weird thing is, he wasn't wearing any. I swear that dude is a magnet.

This makes Sheridan cry.

Audri says, *Jagger!*

— What? I say. Sheridan asked if there was a swarm of girls and there was only one. I thought that would make her happy.

226

Then Sheridan says she's sorry for being so sensitive. She blames the curse because she's usually not the jealous type.

I agree and remind them that when the Rosco's hostess was all over Duffy, Sheridan was cool about it.

Audri looks at me like I messed up again but Sheridan says she's glad I recognized her strength. She's only feeling sensitive because it's been out of control lately. They can't even buy a Big Gulp after school without being stopped ten times. She feels like she's with Kellan friggin' Lutz. She feels like a groupie. And the worst part is, Duffy never tells the girls to go away. It's like he likes the attention.

LIE #55: That's weird.

— It doesn't help that my clothes are tight, Sheridan says.

— They don't look tight, Audri says.

— You're probably bloated, I say. The curse will do that.

— Seriously, Jagger?

LIE #56: It's getting late. I better head back to Randy's for the night feeding.

Audri doesn't try to stop me.

I leave a message for Randy on my way home.

I need a sugar glider ASAP.

(That or a miracle.)

One hour later I get the miracle.

Audri texts. She isn't mad.

She says things like, I know you were just trying to help and it's not your fault you think like a guy and next time I'm having a deep conversation with Sheridan I'll warn you so you can wait until we're done.

227

I want to ask what part of that conversation was deep, but I don't.

I say being a girl seems hard.

She says, you're not kidding.

And I'm not.

That feels good.

Lily

Monday, November 5, 2012

I waited until Duffy left with the dogs before going over. Yes I, Lily Bader-Huffman, wanted to avoid him. That's how mortified I am. And when I think about how he found out...how long he's known...who Mandy might have told...

SHUDDER. CLENCH. CRINGE!

I can't even write about it. It's too soon.

The plan was to get my skateboard and laptop with haste and then live in a cave until graduation. Only that didn't happen. The moment Mandy opened the door I began to sob.

She offered me a seat on the edge of her bed and encouraged me to let it out. I did, with projectile vomit–like force.

"It's the pressure...."

"I know." Mandy placed a hand on my back. "Ew, itchy," she said, removing it. "You need some cashmere in that blend."

"Sorry," I said, not really sure what for. "It's so much harder than I thought. All the rules and expectations. There are literally hundreds of ways to make mistakes and zero ways to correct them."

Her narrow Kate Hudson eyes narrowed even more as she squint-nodded in agreement.

"It's like if we're not perfect we're nothing, you know." I sniffled. "But who's perfect? I mean, everyone tries, but who really is? Why is that even the goal?"

"Wait until you're a junior. It's worse."

"I think that's why I wanted to hang with your brother so badly, you know? Like, if I was with a cool guy I wouldn't feel so..."

"Single?" Mandy said.

I was going to say lost, but single worked too. I sighed. "The anxiety got to me."

"How could it not?" Mandy said. "Our lives are all about GPAs, and practices, and clubs, and fund-raising, and... stress!" She was pacing now, powered by the strength of her conviction. "We should change Advanced Placement classes to Aliminate Pressure classes, because if college is such a fundamental right, shouldn't we get accepted no matter what?"

Did she really think "eliminate" was spelled with an A, that college was a fundamental right, and that I was talking about academic pressure, not social? I could have set her straight, but Mandy Duffy was looking *at* me, not *through* me, and I didn't want that to stop. "*Carpe diem, quam minimum credula postero,*" I said.

"Is that tongues?" she asked.

"Latin," I said. "It means 'Seize the day, trusting little to the future.' It's from a poem by Horace. It's about living in the moment."

"How do you know it?"

"AP English, how else?" I said, as if resentful.

"Can I mention it in my next blog?" she asked.

"Sure," I sniffled. "Call it *Horace Power.*"

Mandy was so grateful for the title she gave me a bottle of gold nail polish and a hug. Both made me feel a tiny bit closer to belonging. They also made me wonder if I've been focused on the wrong Duffy.

Lily Bader-Huffman-Duffy

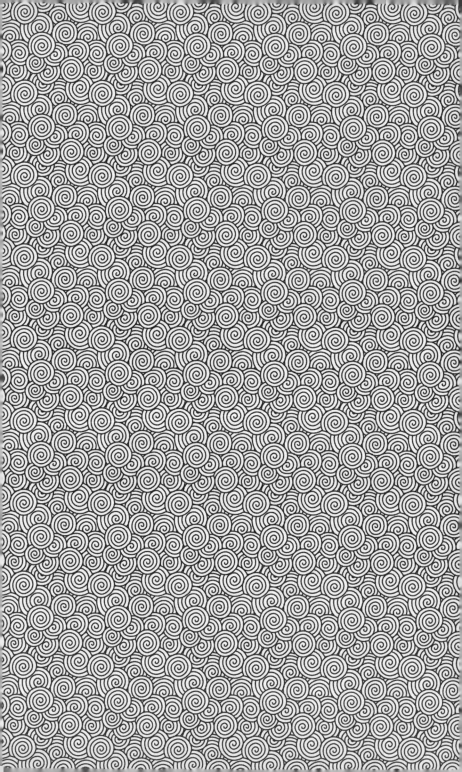

Sheridan

11.5.12

INT. THE SPENCER HOME—KITCHEN FLOOR—NIGHT.

SHERIDAN sits on the cold tiles and watches her cinnamon crescent rolls bake. Her head appears twisted in the oven's aluminum finish; a distortion of her looks, but a true reflection of how she feels.

The one time I don't want an audience and—*ta-da!*— there's Jagger. Audri should have said *Tonight's showing of* Sheridan's Superlatively Pathetic Life *isn't open to the public*, but she offered him a front-row seat instead.

So there I am Meryl Weeping about everything, and rather

than offering some cool male perspective, Jagger says I look bloated. And you know what Audri says? She says, *Seriously*.

The whole thing makes me want to B.U.R.B.F. Because when you Become UR own Best Friend you send a message to the world that says, *I am president of my own fan club, I keep my own secrets, and I am constantly channeling the lyrics from Christina Aguilera's song "Beautiful." Did you hear that, people? Words can't bring me down!*

The oven is buzzing! What do you know? My crescent rolls have risen and so have my spirits. Time to channel a Chinese dog and chow.

TAKE FIVE.

CUT.

INT. THE SPENCER HOME—KITCHEN BAR—TWENTY MINUTES LATER.

SHERIDAN licks her cinnamon-flavored fingers, then puts quill to paper.

Audri just texted to apologize for dropping the Jagger-bomb on me. I responded with a B.U.R.B.F.-inspired *All good* and a thumbs-up emoji. She said I sounded much better and wanted to know why. I said I'd fill her in tomorrow. I think she feels threatened by my newfound independence, because she's bringing me a chai latte for our walk to school and usually she only brings one for herself.

SHERIDAN puts down her quill and high-fives herself. Her phone rings. It's DUFFY.

Hello?

Hey.

Hey. (Me.) In my best I'm-not-at-all-bummed-about-the-Big-Gulp-incident voice. *What's up?*

Nothing. Just walking Fleas Navidad and Saint Tick.

Those names crack me up so I laugh. Then I stop and it's quiet.

Hello? (Me.)

Hey.

Oh, I thought you hung up or something.

Why?

I didn't hear anything.

Oh.

More silence. It's awkward. I begin to wonder if he regrets calling me . . . then why he called me in the first place . . . then why he hasn't called sooner. . . .

I lick the icing off the last crescent roll.

Did you hear anything about your audition? (Duffy.)

No. I'm kind of freaking.

I was like that after I tried out for the Flames.

Really?

Yeah.

But you made it.

You will too. (Duffy, competing with my crescent roll icing for sweetest thing ever.) *You have my lucky ring, remember.*

(Gulp.)

Unless you gave that one to Audri too.

Ha! Nope. (Me, freaking.) *Where did you get it, anyway? My brothers want one.*

236

For some reason this made Duffy very happy. He gave me the web address and even a promo code. I thanked him and then said I was going to hang up and order them right away.

Wait, before you go. (Duffy.) *I was wondering if you want to hang out sometime? You know, just us.*

Sure. (Me, trying not to sound excited.)

Cool. (Duffy, trying not to sound excited.) *Saturday? Like a movie or something?*

I squealed with delight when we hung up. I was about to call my best friend and tell her the news when I realized she was already here.

CUE SOUND EFFECT:

Awwwwww.

To Be Continued . . .

END SCENE.

DUFFY

Monday

I'm outside with Fleas Navidad and Saint Tick (Hud came up with those names) when I see Lily leaving my house. I hide behind the car until she's gone. Then I run inside, close the shades, and run up to Mandy's room.

The sign on her door says CAREFUL OR YOU'LL END UP IN MY BLOG. She hangs it there whenever she's working on a post. She says interruptions throw her.

Feeling = I don't care if I throw her or not. I'm going in.

ME: What was Lily doing here?

MANDY: Helping Mom fold your underwear.

ME: *What?*

MANDY: Hashtag kidding. She left a few things here by accident.

ME: *Accident?*

Feeling = If I was the kind of dude who made air quotes, I would have made them there.

ME: Mandy, you can't fall for her excuses. She's a psycho.

MANDY: *Was* a psycho. She's over all that.

ME: How do you know?

MANDY: She told me.

ME: You know how honest psychos are.

MANDY: She was telling the truth. Trust me. I read people the way you read . . . cereal boxes.

Feeling = I love reading cereal boxes while I'm eating breakfast. Word searches are my favorite.

ME: Keep her away from me. That girl has crazy in her eyes.

MANDY: She just needs some mascara. I think she's one makeover away from serious potential. Do you know she speaks Latin?

ME: Do you know I just farted on your pillow?

MANDY: Gross!

She whipped a magazine at me. It smelled like old-lady perfume. I whipped it back.

MANDY: How are you ever going to find a girlfriend?

ME: Um, no problems there.

Feeling = I wanted to pour hot sauce in my own mouth for

saying something that slick. But Mandy thinks she's the only hot Duffy, and she's not. I have three S's: Sheridan, Screamers, and a Stalker! All she has is a boyfriend named Gardner and random dudes who stare.

MANDY: When's the last time you went on a date? Or should I say, when's the first time you went on a date?

ME: I happen to have something lined up this weekend.

MANDY: Laser tag with Hud and Coops doesn't count.

ME: Try a movie with Sheridan Spencer.

MANDY: @AndrewDuffy43 is taking @Sheridan_Star on a date? She's legitimately cute.

Feeling = Who talks like that??

MANDY: Wait. I don't believe you. When?

ME: Saturday night.

MANDY: Better change that to Friday.

ME: Can't. We play Pinedale.

MANDY: Better cancel, then. Amelia's coming home from Barnard Saturday, remember?

ME: This Saturday?

MANDY: Like I said, you'll never find a girlfriend.

—LATER

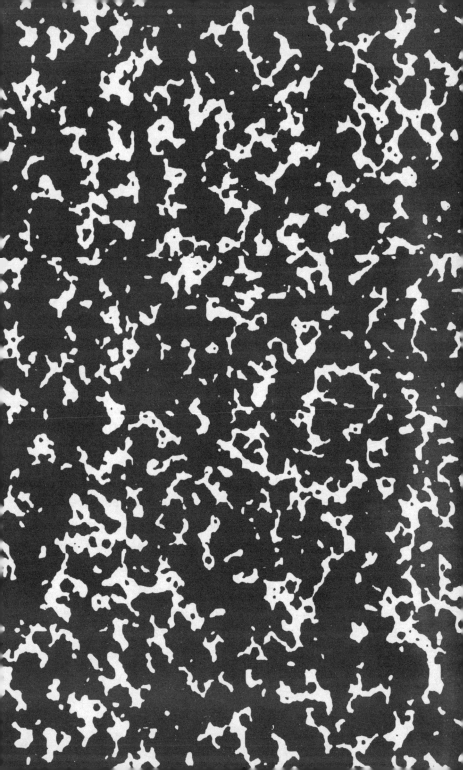

Sheridan

Literally two minutes after I spoke to Duffy.

INT. THE SPENCER HOME—KITCHEN.

SHERIDAN asks her FATHER for his Visa so she can get a jump on her holiday shopping. He agrees that the Toolery rings would be perfect for MAX and HENRY. In fact, he thinks his salesmen and VIP customers will like them too. He asks SHERIDAN to order twenty.

I was starting to think my run of bad luck was over until Duffy called back to cancel our date. He claims his sister will be home from college for one night, but I don't believe him.

I think he told his buddies about us and they told him he was crazy for tying himself down. They probably reminded him that he has much better options, and he agreed.

So you know what I did? I called his bluff and said I'd love to meet his sister. He sounded surprised and he stammered a bit, but eventually he said okay.

Now I'm freaking out because I think I just forced him to hang with me and he clearly doesn't want to. Cheeses! I was more confident when Duffy and I were just friends. Now that he likes me I'm totally insecure. Now what do I do? Call him back? Text? Call Audri? I know I should ask my inner BF, but she's just as flummoxed as I am.

To Be Continued...

END SCENE.

Lily

Tuesday, November 6, 2012

Who's the stalker now?

I always knew Mike was possessive so I've been sending his calls directly to voice jail; do not pass go, do not collect two hundred dollars. Because he's the kind of guy who will go back to stink-eyeing me the minute Blake's gay break is over.

But tonight Mike played dirty and called the house phone. Mom, thinking he was a potential suitor, insisted I take the call.

"Seriously?" he said when I picked up. "Why have you been ignoring me?"

"Why have you been harassing me?"

"Lilian!" Mom snapped.

I locked myself in the upstairs bathroom and ran the shower.

"I'm harassing you because I need my blazer back."

"As soon as you return that hour I wasted with you at the mall."

"I'm not kidding, Lily."

"Neither am I, Mike. We had a deal. Anyway, I don't have it anymore."

"*What?* Where is it?"

"I gave it to Blake."

"*Why?*"

"I thought it would make him miss you."

"Ohgodohgodohgod," he mumbled. "What did he say?"

"He wasn't home. I left a note that said: Inhale the cheap cologne on this collar. Remember who you are. Remember who you love. Remember to call me. I have life-changing news."

"It's not cheap—it's Calvin Klein," Mike said. And then, "Did he call you?"

"No. But he will."

I expected Mike to thank me for my efforts, but all he said was, "Just get it back, okay?" Then the line went dead.

Thank god for Algebra homework. It's the only thing left in my world that still makes sense.

Lily Bader-Huffman-Duffy

Vanessa

November 7th

Forgive me, Journal, for I have sinned. It has been three days since my last entry. Like you, I expected my first kiss with Blake to inspire elegantly crafted musings on young love that I would name *Food Court Courting*. But alas, my hands[96] have been far too shaky to control a pen, due to a major oversight on my part.

Making the first move on Blake was a massive error. Obvious reasons[97] aside, I forgot that forcing Lily to witness our

---

[96] I said "hands" and not "hand" because I am ambidextrous.

[97] 1. Blake's kiss was stiff and cold. My lips felt like they were stuck to a frozen pole. 2. I hate when A.J. is right. 3. Blake has not tried to kiss

passion would stoke her jealousy fire. Thusly, leading to more snail-mail threats and eventually turning me in. Hence, my three-day battle with shaking paranoia.

Then Blake shows up today wearing her ill-fitting blazer, and I know she has weaseled her way back in. Simply put, I was losing, and losing makes me itch. So now I'm itchy and shaking, which makes it hard to scratch with precision. By lunch I had a hole in my blouse.

I told Blake I was embarrassed by the hole and asked if I could wear his blazer. Mostly because I needed another layer between my nails and skin, but also to see if he cared enough about me to upset Lily.

Journal, I know what you're thinking—Vanessa let her ego and unequivocal need to win get in the way of her better judgment—*again!*—thusly creating another opportunity for Lily to seek revenge.

And you know what, Journal, you would be right, if the moment[98] I put on said ill-fitting blazer hadn't provided me with enough evidence to shut Lily down. But it did.

So you're not right, Journal. You're wrong. I'm right.

------

me since. 4. He has declined all recent invitations to study together. 5. He swears everything is fine and that he's just not big on PDA, yet his public display of hand-holding borders on obsessive.

[98] Hyperbole. I didn't find the note until bedtime.

Lily

Thursday, November 8, 2012

A sudden *thunk* woke me up. Then silence. The world was unusually quiet for 11:18 AM. *Eleven eighteen!!!* I shot out of bed in a panic and stepped on a note from Mom.

Don't panic. I shut off your alarm. Snow day.

I started to think about all the work I could have done if I had known about this: two more hours last night, six more this morning... when I heard another *thunk*.

I expected to find a Rorschach of bird guts and feathers on my window but saw Blake Marcus instead. Like a snow-globe figurine, he was dressed in festive J.Crew outerwear, which included but was not limited to a faux-fur hat with dangling pom-poms and red lace-up boots. He was standing next to an igloo with a blue spray-painted peace sign on top.

I closed the blinds and went back to bed.

Lily Bader-Huffman-Duffy

Lily

Thursday, November 8, 2012

Kidding. I was so excited I hurried downstairs in my pajamas, threw two mugs of instant hot chocolate in the microwave, and ran outside in Dad's puffy coat and Mom's Sasquatch boots.

"What are you wearing?" Blake asked, like the whole Pub-fart thing never happened.

"How'd you get so tanned?"

"Windburn."

"Good," I said, handing him a mug. "I hope it ages you prematurely."

"Igloo?"

I nodded. He led the way.

Outdoor survival had been one of the many things we learned as Homies. The interior flair—including but not limited to fold-out chairs, Navaho throws, and sheepskin rug—was all Blake. "What do you think?"

We were sitting knee-to-knee sipping our hot chocolates, but I still couldn't warm to him. My anger needed another minute to thaw.

"Blake," I finally said. "Mandy told everyone you're gay, not me, and not Duffy."

"But you told Duffy. A guy you didn't even know. A guy who doesn't even—"

"A guy who doesn't even like me back?"

He shrugged like you-said-it-I-didn't. I wanted to throw my mug at his face.

"I'm sorry I betrayed you. I feel terrible," I said. "Tell me, Blake. How do you handle the guilt?"

"What guilt?"

"Betraying a friend."

"Huh?" he said.

"You know, leading Vanessa on."

"How am I leading her on?"

"Oh please. Hand-holding during lunch, hand-holding between classes, making out at the mall!"

"She told you that?"

"I was there, Blake. I saw you. I was having lunch with Mike. You remember him, right? The guy you were in love with before you took a break from gay?"

"Did he see?"

"No, I distracted him," I said. "For his sake, not yours."

"Thank you," he muttered. His brown eyes looked hard, dull.

"That's what ex–best friends are for," I joked.

Neither one of us laughed.

I lowered my eyes and fussed with the fringe on my blanket. "I'm sorry I told Duffy."

"I'm sorry I ignored you like that."

I looked up. Tears rolled down. "You are?"

"I miss you, Lil. The second I smelled that blazer and read your note . . . I . . ."

"I *knew* that would get you," I sparked.

Blake sighed. "I'm pathetic, aren't I?"

"Yeah."

"So are you," he said.

"I know."

"Now what?"

"You could start by taking a break from straight," I said.

"If you take a break from outing me."

"If you take a break from having Coxsackie."

"If you take a break from giving it to me."

"If you take a break from—"

"Shhh." Blake's smile fell. "Did you hear that?"

Pant, sniff, stab, slide. Pant, sniff, stab, slide. Pant, sniff, stab, slide . . .

We leaned toward the opening of the igloo, but not close

enough to see anything for fear of being spotted. As the rhythm grew louder we leaned even closer.

We exchanged a wide-eyed gaze. *What is that?*

I needed to know. Silently, I counted to three.

One . . . two . . . When I got to *three* I shoved Blake out. He landed tanned-face-first in the snow.

"How unequivocally stupid do you think I am?" shouted a girl's voice. She was shuffling toward us on cross-country skis. Her red snow jacket and matching pants were stuffed full of so many layers her torso took on the shape of an egg. When I spotted her white mittens I couldn't resist.

"It's a peanut M&M," I whispered to Blake.

"Shhh," Blake hissed. Then he stood. "Vanessa?"

Uh-oh.

She lifted her ski goggles. "Did you really think I wouldn't find out?"

Blake hurried to her. "I'm so sorry. I wasn't trying to—"

Vanessa pushed past him. "Not you," she snapped. *"Her!"*

"Me?"

"Stop the innocent act, Lily."

"What did I do?"

We were standing in a triangle, the literary significance of which was not lost on me. But when snow is squalling and accusations are flying, it's best to keep these observations to oneself.

"I found the note. So go ahead, turn me in for upgrading. I'll turn you in for extortion."

253

"Extortion?" Blake snickered. *"Lily?"*

"Vanessa, do you even know what extortion means? Because if you did you wouldn't accuse me of—"

"Ugh!" Vanessa stomped her ski. "You two are so pretentious. You think you're better than everyone because you were homeschooled."

"Ha!"

"Better than everyone?" Blake added. "Um, no."

"Well, some of us have to study to get A's. Some of us have to *try*. And some of us are stupid enough to think you really liked me."

"Is this about me or Blake?"

That's when she showed us the note.

The question isn't if *all will be revealed. It's* <u>when</u> . . .

"You think I wrote that?" I asked.

"You're the only one who knows what I did, and I happened to find it in *your* blazer."

"That's not Lily's blazer," Blake said. "It's Mike's."

"But you told me it was—"

"Yeah." Blake sighed. "I told you a lot of things."

Vanessa threw down her poles. "I'm so confused." She buried her face in her mittens.

"I think we all are," I said, leading her into the igloo.

It was the perfect opportunity for Blake to tell Vanessa the truth, but he didn't. Normally, I would have found pleasure in his discomfort, hoping it might bring him closer to a confession. But I needed to prove I'd never betray him again, so I turned the attention back to me.

"Why would I want to threaten you?"

"Because Blake and I are a thing," she said, "and you obviously have feelings for him."

"Vanessa, I don't, I swear."

"Then why didn't you respond to the email I sent last week?"

"I was using a typewriter."

"Aha!" Vanessa said.

"What?"

"The notes were typed. Case closed."

"Wait," I said, finally understanding why Mike was so desperate to get his blazer back. "Doesn't Mike have a typewriter?"

"Yeah," Blake said. "He bought it at a garage sale during his *Mad Men* phase."

"Mike wrote that note, Vanessa. Not me."

"Mike? Why would Mike?" Vanessa asked, searching us both for something that made sense. "Lily, did you tell him what I did?"

I glared at Blake. *Handle this.*

Blake glared back. *Don't make me do this.*

Finally, he said, "Mike can be a little . . . jealous."

"I *knew* he liked me," Vanessa said. "Don't worry, though. He's hardly a threat."

"More like he likes *me*," Blake said.

"Huh?" Vanessa knit her brows while her hard drive calculated this new route. "Wait. You mean . . . Mike is gay?"

"Yes," Blake said.

"But . . ." Vanessa paused.

Blake lowered his eyes.

"Oh," she said flatly. Then she turned to me. "Did you know?"

I nodded and braced myself for the icy stab of her ski pole.

She sighed. "That's a relief."

"It is?" Blake asked.

"I thought there was something wrong with me."

We spent the rest of the afternoon laughing about misunderstandings, embarrassing truths, and how hard it was to pretend we hadn't missed one another.

When Mom surprised us with a fresh round of steaming hot chocolates, we lifted our mugs and toasted many things, including but not limited to: homosexuals, stalkers, upgrading perfectionists, the magic of snow days, second chances, and peanut M&M's who ski.

Lily Bader-Huffman-Duffy

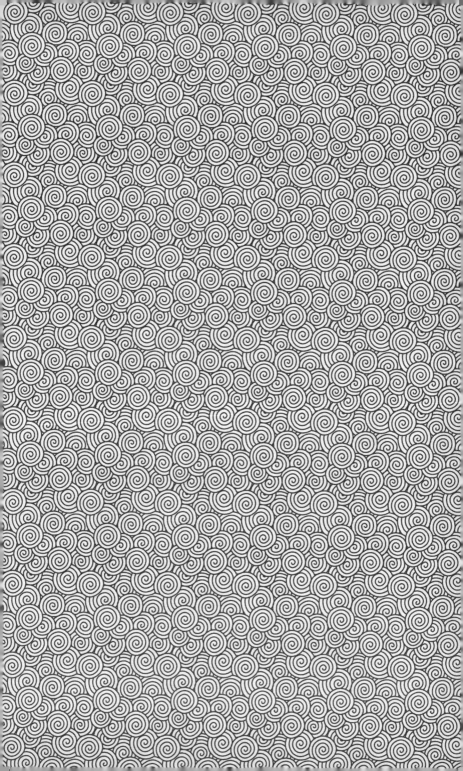

DUFFY

Friday

The Flames were on fire tonight, especially for an away game. We smoked the Pinedale Gulls 66–32.

I wore my old sweatbands under my Heavy Metal Bands so I don't know which bands brought the luck. Maybe wearing both at the same time did it. Maybe that's why everything is so doubly epic right now.

At first the Gulls called us Team Wonder Woman because we all had them. But by the end of the game they were asking where we got them because the Pinedale girls were all over us, trying to touch and feel the cuffs up close.

Feeling = Hud said that's the excuse they gave their

boyfriends. And that they were all over us because they thought we were hot.

I wasn't sure if he was right until I asked this girl who looked like Katy Perry where we should go for a slice.

GIRL: Cuts. The Brick House is always crowded.

I didn't mean "we" as in me and her. I meant it as in me and the Flames. But my guys were fist-bumping so I said cool.

Feeling = I'm glad Sheridan wasn't there. Not because I liked these girls more than I liked her. I didn't. But I *did* like that they liked me and I didn't feel like pretending I didn't.

Morty, our bus driver, followed Katy Perry's car to Cuts. Tons of her hot friends showed up and we took over the whole restaurant. Everyone was laughing and taking stupid pics with each other's phones and having fun until the Gulls showed up.

I didn't mind because I moved a ton of product. The guys on my team were pretty pissed, though.

First thing I did when I got home was check my sales.

Feeling = When did Mr. Spencer buy 20 Toolery rings?

Feeling = Sheridan rocks!

$533.85 to go.

Feeling = No problem.

— LATER

Sheridan

11.10.12

INT. THE SPENCER HOME—PANTRY FLOOR—NIGHT.

Nude and swaddled in last year's pink Christmas Snuggie, SHERIDAN channels herself from the year 1997, back when she was a fetus in utero and still a size zero.

Heavy sigh.

SHERIDAN lifts her gaze toward the cabinets overhead. How proud they seem, storing our favorite snacks, juice boxes, and nonperishables. But behind their glossy finish lies an aching sadness.

I know this, Pantry, because I too have been unfairly

judged. Me by my society, you by Mom when guests stop by. *Ashley, I just love what you've done with the kitchen. What's behind that door, another bathroom?*

Storage. Come, let me show you the den.

Mom doesn't like that you're L-shaped and thinks a D or a T would be more practical. Well, you know what I don't like, Mom? Shapeists! And unfortunately for me and Christina Aguilera and Pantry, people like you walk among us.

FLASHBACK.

INT. THE DUFFY HOME—LIVING ROOM—EVENING.

I prepared for the role of "parent-approved love interest" by workshopping my smile, handshake, and costume—dark-wash jeans, floral blouse (untucked), and winter-white blazer. I researched conversation topics like Thursday's snowstorm, *The Life of Pi*—movie vs. book—and Lady Gaga's new tattoo. I even brought homemade pralines. Did I sneak two in the car ride over? Yes. Yes I did. That's how superlatively nervous I was.

Mom sensed my anxiety because she went into a whole story about the first time Dad introduced her to Grammy and Grandpa. I nodded like I was listening, but it was impossible to hear over the noise inside my head.

Is Duffy dreading my arrival? What did they say about me during dinner? What if they don't like pralines? Why didn't I ask about nut allergies? Does Amelia even exist? If so, is she even more beautiful than Mandy? If so, how ugly will I look by comparison?

I took it as a good sign when Duffy answered the door. The dogs charged me, and then began obsessing over the zipper of my jeans. I pretended to pet them but was really pushing them away from my First Lady.

Finally, someone normal. (Duffy, smiling.)

(Me, looking over my shoulder.) *Where?*

He laughed. I blushed. He was wearing worn jeans, a green shirt with duct tape over the logo, and socks. No gold cuffs or designer denim. More like how he used to dress when we first met. Another good sign.

Are you sure you want to do this? (Duffy.)

Why? You don't want me to?

I do. Do you?

Yeah.

Close the door, it's freezing! (Mandy.)

Maybe if you had more body fat you wouldn't be so cold. (Amelia?)

Maybe if you had less you wouldn't be so jealous. (Mandy.)

Girls, please. I could die any minute. Don't make this the last thing I hear.

I love you, Bubbie. (Amelia.)

I love you more. (Mandy.)

Better.

Duffy asked if I wanted to leave my cookies with my coat, like they were shopping bags or something.

I brought them for dessert.

You can eat that much? (He asked.)

They're for your family, not me.

(He looked confused.) *We already had dessert.*

262

You're such a guy. (Me.) *The girls will appreciate it. You'll see.*

He shrugged and then led me into the living room to meet his sister. The whole family was there. Lazing by the fire, flipping through magazines, and dressed in pajamas. Even Mr. Duffy, who upon seeing me announced that he was going upstairs to read.

Everyone else looked at me like I was some vagrant who wandered in through an open door. *Hi, I'm Sheridan.*

Mrs. Duffy, a blond celery with navy eyes that matched her nightgown, said, *I'm Patricia. If we knew Andrew was having company we wouldn't be dressed like this.*

I managed to shake her hand without dropping my plate.

Duff—Andrew didn't tell you I was coming over? Speaking his real name felt awkward, like it was made of marbles instead of sounds.

I thought I did. (Duffy.) If he hadn't blushed I never would have believed him.

Andrew, what happened to Lily? (Bubbie Libby.)

Ma! (Patricia.)

Bubbie! (Duffy.)

What? I liked her.

Well, any girl who brings pralines has my vote. I'm Amelia.

She was nowhere as pretty as Mandy. Not because she couldn't be, but because she wasn't trying to be. Her stringy hair was dyed black, possibly to match her outfit and chipped nail polish. Green eyes were her only pop of color. She was Mandy on opposite day.

I offered her the plate. She took three pralines and thanked me with a kind smile.

Anyone else?

No thanks. (Mandy while chexting.)

Mrs. Duffy fake-yawned. *None for me, thanks. I'm off to bed.*

I wanted to offer some to Bubbie Libby but I didn't know what to call her. She wasn't my "Bubbie" and I hadn't been cleared for "Libby" so all I said was, *Any for you?*

She leaned closer to the plate. The tops of her boobs spilled from her nightgown. *Are they kosher?*

They are. (Me, proudly.)

She looked impressed and then pinched one off the plate.

You have a kosher kitchen? (Amelia.)

I'm not sure. I looked at Duffy. *Do I?*

Doubt it.

The praline came to a complete stop at the pucker in Bubbie Libby's lips.

Why would you say they're kosher if you're not sure?

What happened next was the closet thing to stage fright I had ever experienced. Blushing, sweating, shaky voice, dry mouth, confusion, delayed responses, awkward pauses. *I thought—doesn't kosher mean good? You know, like everything's kosher over here.*

Mandy busted out laughing. *Classic!*

Bubbie Libby tossed the praline on the plate, then looked at Duffy like this was his fault.

He ignored her and asked if I wanted to go downstairs and watch TV.

I said okay even though all I really wanted to do was go home and punch my pillow.

Andrew, help me upstairs, will you please? (Bubbie Libby.)

Why?

My sciatica.

Your what?

Now!

Mandy hurried to her feet and ran from the room.

Don't you dare steal the remote! (Duffy, following Bubbie Libby up the stairs.) *Mandy! I'm serious. Don't.*

So now it's just me, Amelia, and the pralines. I take two and bite into both at once.

I'm impressed. (Amelia.)

Why?

You have substance. I can tell.

Thanks. (Me, finally smiling.)

I always thought my kid brother would be more into girls like Mandy. You know—textbook pretty, living off all-you-can-tweet buffets and celebrity sound bites.

Thanks. Amelia was obviously clever and I felt honored to have won her seal of approval.

But you're more like me. You don't have to be the hottest girl in the room because that's not what you're about. You don't beat your-self up because you're ten pounds heavier than everyone else. I'm the same way. And I have to say, I'm impressed that Andrew is com-fortable with that. It says a lot about him.

Good. (Me.) *I left something in the car. Be right back.*

I tossed the plate in their bushes and ran. Tears blurred my vision. Cold air bit my lungs. Snot bubbled from my nose. I didn't care. I kept running.

Mom gasped when I came in the door. She hugged me and asked me what happened. I cried so hard I threw up.

Don't worry. I hated it.

To Be Continued . . .

END SCENE.

Lily

Saturday, November 10, 2012

<u>My View in Haiku.</u>

Blondie goes next door (5)
Baked goods on a plate for him (7)
Too happy to care. (5)

By Lily Bader-Huffman.

Duffy

Sunday

I have no clue why Sheridan left my house without saying goodbye. I wanted to go after her, but Bubbie Libby said it's for the best. Once a runner, always a runner. I said she's not a runner. Maybe something happened.

BUBBIE: She tried to poison me, that's what happened.

Feeling = Bubbie only wants me to date Jewish girls. So I asked my sisters.

MANDY: Amelia called her fat.

AMELIA: You weren't even there.

MANDY: That's what you think.

AMELIA: You were eavesdropping?

MANDY: Reporting.

AMELIA: Well then, you should know I didn't call her fat. I complimented her on being comfortable in her own skin.

ME: What does that mean?

AMELIA: It means starvation isn't her hobby and I said I admired that.

MANDY: Exactly. Who wants to hear that?

AMELIA: Sane people.

ME: It wasn't the fat thing. She doesn't care about that stuff.

MANDY: Every girl cares.

ME: Not Sheridan. She's cool.

AMELIA: Then go find her. Any decent man would.

MANDY: Don't.

ME: Why?

MANDY: Because you're freshman A-list. If anyone finds out you're chasing after some drama queen you'll lose status. Would you rather be decent or respected?

ME: Decent.

Amelia clapped.

BUBBIE LIBBY (from upstairs): Respected!

Mandy clapped.

Feeling = I wanted to go after Sheridan. I wanted to be decent and make sure she was okay.

Feeling = I want to be respected because I know what it feels like not to be, and it's worse than getting kicked in the tenders.

MANDY: Sheridan's the rude one, not you. She's the one who left without saying goodbye.

Bubbie Libby (from upstairs) started clapping.

I ended up watching *SNL* and passing out until 3 AM. When I woke up I checked my phone. No texts. No messages from her parents either, so I guess she made it home.

Feeling = I guess I'll see her at school.

— LATER

Jagger

Nov. 11.

I open my eyes.

There's a shadowy figure sitting in the chair beside my bed.

He's wearing a suit.

I'm being taken downtown for questioning.

I hope I get time to pee and put in my contacts before we go.

I wonder which lie gave me away.

I contemplate the drop from my bedroom window. A real neck-breaker, a hip at the very least.

I can't do it. I don't like hospital smells.

I put on my glasses.

I flop back onto my pillow.

It's just a suit. No man inside. Mother must have put it there.

I wonder if someone died.

Then I remember.

It's Ponnowitz holiday card photo day.

I'd be happier if someone died.

Sheridan

11.11.12

INT. THE SPENCER HOME—PANTRY FLOOR—MORNING.

SHERIDAN wakes up on the pantry floor to the sound of her MOTHER's voice on the telephone. She was talking to MADELON ETIENNE.

I GOT IT. I GOT IT. I GOT IT. I GOT IT. I GOT IT. I GOT IT. I GOT IT. I GOT IT. I GOT IT. I GOT IT. I GOT IT. I GOT IT. I GOT IT. I GOT IT. I GOT IT. I GOT IT. I GOT IT. I GOT IT. DID YOU HEAR THAT B.U.R.B.F.??

I.

GOT.

IT!

I can't wait to tell Audri. I can't wait to tell Octavia! I can't wait to humble-brag it to Mr. Kimble so he can superlatively regret not casting me as Elphaba. Hey, Duffys: You should have eaten my pralines while you had the chance!

Should any of you want to apologize, stop by the studio in early January. I'll be playing an au pair in a variety show called *Amuse-Bouche*.

What, Duffys? You're too uncouth to know what those French words mean? Allow me to translate.

An au pair is what the French call a nanny or governess. Surely you've heard of *Mary Poppins*, no? That's right, Andrew, I did play her a few summers ago, nice of you to remember. Why yes, there is a video available upon request.

Amuse-Bouche translates to *Mouth Amuser*. Is this "mouth amuser" kosher? Good question, Bubbie Libby. Madelon said they're still working on the American title so why don't you hold off for now. I'll know more when I go in to sign my contract on the 30th.

Gotta go. Mom and I are going jogging. Catch me if you can!

SPOILER ALERT:

You can't.

To Be Continued . . .

END SCENE.

Jagger

Nov. 11.

Garron is our family photographer.

He speaks with an Italian accent, but I know for a fact he was born on Long Island. He thinks we should change things up this year.

I say, how about we don't do this.

My brothers laugh.

Father says, Matthew! Benjamin! Don't encourage him.

Then Mother says she'd like to hear Garron's thoughts.

His big revelation? Mother and Father should stand *behind* their sons this year, not beside them. Everything else—our matching navy suits and green-checked shirts, Mother's green-checked dress, and Noodle's green-checked bow—is *bellissimo*!

The way I see it, nothing will be *bellissimo* unless Garron Photoshops prison bars over our faces.

Since that's not going to happen, I have to make it so I can't be ID'd.

Garron fires off a few test shots to check the composition and lighting.

He's says he's ready.

He asks if we're ready.

We say yes.

He says, smile.

I lower my head.

– Daniel, face toward the camera.

– Daniel, eyes open.

– Head up, Daniel.

– Lower your hands, Daniel.

Mother pinches a warning into my shoulder. It feels like a hawk's talon.

– Lower the dog, Daniel.

– The dog.

– Face away from the dog!

Mom's talon lands again. Daniel, please! It's freezing out here.

LIE #57: Sorry.

– Daniel, look at the lens.

– My lens...the camera's lens!

– Son!

LIE #58: I'm trying!

Garron says we're losing light.

LIE #59 a): I have to go to the bathroom.

LIE #59 b): No, I can't hold it.

LIE #59 c): Yes, I'll hurry.

I don't come back for twenty minutes.

Garron makes us rotate. Something about chasing the sun. We have five minutes left before it sets.

He asks if we're ready.

We say yes.

I unclamp Noodle's leash.

Noodle bolts.

LIE #60: How did that happen?

Father says, forget the dog.

Mother says, that dog is part of this family.

I offer to chase after him.

Garron says it will be dark by the time I get back.

Matthew has a meeting to prep for.

Benjamin has a date.

Garron says he has enough to work with.

He's lying.

Mother sends me to my room for being so difficult.

I say, how old am I, six?

She says I'm acting like it.

I decide to go because resisting arrest is not in my best interest. And I want to journal my lies before I forget.

They let me out for dinner.

Matthew and Benjamin are still there.

So is the Legacy Hygienics shrink.

Mother says Dr. Lloyd is here to lead an intervention.

– Whose? I ask.

– Yours.

– *Mine?*

– Yes, says Father.

– Why?

Dr. Lloyd says my family believes I'm taking drugs. Are you taking drugs, Daniel?

LIE #61: Yes, Dr. Lloyd. I am.

DUFFY

Monday

Sheridan goes the entire day without talking to me.

Feeling = I really want to know why she left my house Saturday night.

So while we're closing up our lockers I update Hud and Coops and ask them what they think I should do.

HUD: If you start kissing up to Sheridan this early on, you'll be whipped by Thanksgiving.

COOPS: He's right.

ME: Who made you guys the experts?

COOPS: Music, dude. It's all right there in the lyrics.

ME: You gotta love One Direction.

COOPS: I'm serious. Who gets more girls than rock stars? No one. They know the deal.

ME: What deal?

HUD: That girls mess with your head.

COOPS: Take Springsteen.

Feeling = It's always about Springsteen with Coops.

ME: The guy's like eighty.

COOPS: He didn't used to be. And all his lyrics are about guys who settled down too early.

ME: What's your point?

COOPS: Don't make the same mistakes Bruce made. Don't settle for one Screamer when you can have them all.

HUD: It's what any self-respecting guy would do.

Feeling = Mandy was right.

It was time for practice so I decided not to think about it anymore.

Two minutes later I see Sheridan outside the theater so I'm thinking about it again.

Feeling = Why did they put the gym and the theater right across from each other? It's not like I'd ever be in a hurry to get from practice to the stage.

ME: Hey, Sheridan, why did you take off on Saturday?

Feeling = It's exactly what I wasn't supposed to do. I couldn't help it. I had to know.

SHERIDAN: No one knew I was coming so I figured no one would mind if I left.

ME: Huh?

SHERIDAN: Forget it. Oh, I got the part.

ME: That's awesome! I knew you would.

SHERIDAN: Yeah, so between that and *Wicked*, I probably won't see you for a while.

Then she turned and walked into the theater, all happy and stuff.

Feeling = Did *she* just end things with *me*?

I sucked in practice.

Feeling = My insides were so heavy I could barely shoot.

The guys asked what was wrong.

I said I just ended things with Sheridan. She cried. I hate when girls cry.

Coops told me to download *The River*.

I listened to Gotye instead.

— LATER

Lily

Tuesday, November 13, 2012

Horace Power went live last night. I feel like a complete Homie snob saying this, but Mandy did much better than I expected and today everyone was tweeting their favorite passages.

Seize the day, not the A! #HoracePower

Too much time preparing for life, not enough time living it. #HoracePower

Can't afford to make mistakes? I say, you can't afford not to. That's how we learn. #HoracePower

Why memorize when you can think? #HoracePower

When someone says "Use your brain," respond with "No time. Too much homework." #HoracePower

Granted, I did several rewrites and was responsible for spinning a Gap idea into a Gucci gown (Mandy's words, not mine), but she calls me *partner* and that's more than I ever expected. She's even naming her dogs Gap and Gucci after us.

I shared this during lunch. Blake thinks I have a girl crush. Vanessa said a girl crush is better than being a stalker. We all agreed.

Wait, it gets better.

Bubbie Libby was sitting on the porch swing when I got home from school.

"Shalom, Lily," she says.

"Shalom," I say with a trace of suspicion. I mean, the woman fired me a few weeks ago and now she's all *Shalom, Lily*? But the definition of the word is three-pronged. It means hello, goodbye, and peace. And maybe, just maybe, she's going for peace. "Aren't you cold?"

"Keeps me from aging," she says. "Messes with my Raynaud's, though."

"Sorry to hear that," I say.

"So, what do you say? You want your dog-walking job back? It would really help me out."

I told her I had too much homework and politely declined. I didn't want Duffy to think I was stalking.

"But we're Jews, Lily. We can never forget that."

"I won't."

"Then say yes," Bubbie Libby said. "If not for me or the dogs, then do it for our people." She put her hands together in prayer.

I wasn't sure when dog walking became a symbol of Judaic faith, but I said okay.

Ten minutes later Duffy and I collided on his front porch. The dog leashes got wrapped around our legs and next thing I know I'm twirling and justifying all at once.

"It's cool," he said. "I believe you."

I quickly righted the dogs and stepped onto the lawn. "Test me. Leave your backpack on the porch, then check it after I leave. Everything will be there. I promise." Then I hurried down the sidewalk dragging Gap and Gucci behind me.

"Let's go," I said, tugging. "You can pee in a minute."

Duffy jogged up beside me. "Is it okay if I go with you?"

I let the dogs pee. "Why?"

He looked up at the bloated gray clouds. "It's about to snow."

"How do you know?"

"Everything feels kind of still and buzzy at the same time. I like it."

I agreed. Not because I'm a stalker, but because I was thinking that too.

I offered Duffy a leash. "Want one?"

He took Gap.

"How did you find out?" he asked. "You know, that I knew you were..."

"Stalking?"

He smiled shyly. "Yeah."

"Mandy told me."

"Figures."

"She didn't tell me *how* you knew. I figured that out on my own." Suddenly, the story I couldn't bear to write became a story I couldn't wait to tell. I wanted to Heimlich it out of my body, spit it on the side of the road, and let the snow cover it up forever. "I happened to be wearing your shoelace as a bracelet when Mandy told me. I was so ashamed I cut it off and threw it in the trash—"

"You could have given it back," Duffy said, smiling.

"Impossible. I never wanted to bother you again." We stopped to let Gucci sniff a hedge. "Also, I ended up feeling sad for the lace so I pulled it out of the trash."

"Sad?"

"I thought it would be happier with the rest of your stuff."

"Ahhh," he said, knowing where this was going.

"So I reach into the very back of my closet and what do I find? Two hard dog poops. Now I know where that smell had been coming from, but I have no idea what they were doing there in the first place, so I asked my mom if any dogs have been in my room lately. And she tells me about the night Gap and Gucci ran into the house and how you found them in my closet."

"They picked up the scent of my stuff," he said, bending down to thank them.

"Yep. And the rest, as they say, is pathetic."

The streetlights popped on.

"Can I ask you something?" Duffy said.

"Sure."

"Why me?"

The first flakes of snow began to fall.

"You seemed so . . . normal."

"Normal?" He sounded insulted. "That's it?"

"You weren't homeschooled. You didn't ride a skateboard to school in the rain. You didn't have a head full of useless facts and a sack full of kosher luncheon meat. You didn't use type-writers or encyclopedias. No one would describe your looks as 'interesting' or your hobbies as 'odd.' You have a popular sister, you play a popular sport, you have popular facial features, friends with cool nicknames, and you don't accessorize with highlighter. So yes, normal."

"I don't get it," he said.

"I thought if I could be close to your *things* I'd get closer to you. And if I was closer to *you* I'd be closer to being *kissed* by you. And if my first *kiss* came from you I'd be magically trans-formed into normal and—Whoa!" Duffy's face fell toward my cheek. "Are you okay?"

He blinked his eyes open. He looked confused, disoriented.

"Do you need a doctor?"

"No," he snapped. Then he stepped closer, and in a gentler tone said, "I'm trying to kiss you."

"Oh." I took a step back. "You don't have to do that. I'm over it. I swear. It's like the spell was broken and—*poof!*—my obsession is gone. Anyway, aren't you and Sheridan a thing?"

"I broke up with her today," he said.

"Oh, I'm sorry."

"No, it's good."

We walked the rest of the way in silence. When we got back to his house he snapped his fingers and said, "Gone? Just like that your obsession is *gone?*"

"Gone." I smiled reassuringly. "I promise, you have nothing to fear. The whole thing was immature. Illusory. I do think your friend Owen is cute, though."

"Coops?"

"He's been saying hi to me lately. Maybe you could put in a good word, you know, now that you know I'm not dangerous." We stepped onto his porch and I pointed to his backpack. "See, it's still there."

I thought he would laugh at that, but all he said was, "Good deal."

"Thanks for the pity kiss," I said, handing him Gucci's leash. "That was very sweet."

"That's what friends are for."

"So we're friends now?"

"As long as none of my things go missing."

"The only thing missing from your porch will be me," I said.

And—*poof!*—I was gone.

Lily Bader-Huffman

Duffy

Tuesday

Dad says things like: Tread lightly around women, Andrew. Simple conversations will become minefields if you're not careful. One wrong move and you'll trigger an explosion.

Feeling = Dad's clueless. Maybe girls were like that when he was a kid, but not these days.

These days they run out of houses without saying goodbye and say things like, I don't have time to hang or it was all illusory.

Feeling = Whatever that means.

They stalk you for months and then toss you like a broken shoelace. They say they want you to kiss them and when you do they think you fainted on them. You try again and they say, I like Coops.

Feeling = No Sheridan. No Stalker. I only have one S left— the Screamers.

— LATER

Vanessa

November 14th

A.J. and I left the house after dinner.[99] We had to get out of there. I was scratching my arms like winning lotto tickets and A.J. was one Nirvana song away from blowing out his eardrums.

"Haven't you sold any cars lately?" I asked as he accelerated through a yellow light.

"Three this month. Mr. Spencer is gonna give me a raise if I keep it going through December."

I punched A.J. on the arm. "Are you kidding? That's a shed-load. Why didn't you tell Mom and Dad? We could have—"

---

[99] We didn't even say goodbye to Mom and Dad.

"Nessa, stop."

"Stop what?"

"This whole Beni's thing." He glanced at me, then sighed. "It's pointless."

"How can you say that?"

"Because it is. Same as putting a Band-Aid on a headache, you know?"

"But—"

"But nothing," he said. "I'm selling these cars for me, not them."

I clenched my teeth. "Why can't it be for both?"

"Because I don't like to think about Mom and Dad fighting when I'm at work, okay? It bums me out." His turquoise eyes darkened to navy. "Anyway, it's going to take a lot more than a few nights at Beni's to fix what they've got." He gripped the wheel like he wanted to pull it off its base. "They were fighting about hand soap tonight. Hand soap!"

"I know, but we can't give up." My tears began to fall, hot and unstoppable.

"It's not our fight."

"So you're just going to quit?"

"Not quit, *accept*."

"Accept what? That Mom and Dad are going to get divorced?"

"Accept that we don't have any control over whether they do or not. It's their deal. I'm done wasting energy on it."

"Who *are* you right now?" I sniffled. "You don't even sound like you."

"I've been reading Mom's Deepak Chopra books." He grinned. "Good stuff. You should check him out."[100]

My left eye twitched. "So it's all up to me?"

A.J. pulled into Lily's driveway and put the car in park. "Guess so."

I slammed the door and rolled my wheelie suitcase filled with books and clothes up her walk. I didn't even look back. Looking back slows a racer's time and I didn't have a second to waste.

---

[100] I let that one go. That's how unequivocally upset I was.

Lily

Wednesday, November 14, 2012

When Vanessa called to ask if she could sleep over, I snapped a selfie of me in my lilac hoodie-footie pj's and sent it to Blake.

B, do you think Vanessa will get the irony?

Maybe if they were ironic, but they're not.

I hate you.

You too. xoxo

I stuffed the hoodie-footies in the back of my closet and changed into sweats. I couldn't wait to dish, in HD detail, about my Duffy encounter, and more importantly, my speedy love-recovery. I wanted to hear how she was handling the news about Blake. Like, *really* handling it. I wanted one of us to accidentally fart and then giggle about it for hours.

I knew none of that would happen when she walked into my house with a suitcase full of books and eyes full of tears.

"It's the surströmming, isn't it?" I said, ruing the day Mom created International Cuisine Night. Tonight's delicacy was fermented herring from Sweden. Top notes include rotten eggs, vinegar, and rancid butter. It tastes worse than it smells.

"No. I mean, it is stinky in here but..." Vanessa lowered her head and her shoulders began to shake.

"Oh crap, are you okay?"

Mom hurried into the foyer the instant her sonar picked up Vanessa's sobs. She was still wearing her blond Swedish wig. I was about to chide her when I realized I was still wearing mine.

"Vanessa, right? I'm Nora." She put her arm around Vanessa's shoulders and led her into the den. I hoped the tears blurred Vanessa's vision to the point where she couldn't see the beanstalks of old periodicals that my parents mistook for necessary.

"I am a trained child psychologist," Mom said. "So if you ever want to talk—"

"Really?" Vanessa sniffled.

"Anytime," Mom said.

"How about now?"

Nora knew exactly when to "fix" Vanessa's problems and when to "listen." She helped her understand why parents fight and how, at times, it can even be healthy. Convincing Vanessa that her parents' marriage had zero correlation to her grade point average was a much harder sell. Vanessa insisted that if she aced her tests on Friday, life at home would improve. Then she suggested we hit the books.

"Try to have *some* fun tonight, girls," Mom said. Then she handed Vanessa a yellowed business card and hugged us both.

"Come to my room," I said. "I want to show you something."

Vanessa popped the handle on her suitcase.

"Leave it. You won't need it."

I led her into my bedroom and proudly showed her the T-shirts splayed out on my bed. "Ta-da!"

" 'Seize the Day, Not the A'?" she read.

"Mandy had them made." I beamed. "She's super connected at the mall because of her job. I got one for you."

Vanessa took a step back. "Nah, I'm good."

"You don't want it?"

Deep-conditioned curls smacked the sides of her face as she shook her head no. "I'm not that into the whole *Horace Power* thing."

"Why not?" I asked, slightly offended.

"Ver? It gives people an excuse to be lazy."

"Taking time to enjoy life isn't lazy; it's what we're supposed to do. It's why we have senses. So we can experience the world around us."

"Wrong. We were born with senses so we could escape predators."

"All I'm saying is . . ." *What was I saying? Academic pressure was Mandy's issue, not mine.* Still, it felt good to speak out about something that Pub kids cared about. "I'm saying we need to stop obsessing over achievements."

"And do what?"

"I don't know. Laugh, explore, experience boredom."

Vanessa pursed her lips and considered this. "I'd rather have the A." Then she asked if I'd help her with her suitcase.

"We have a few days to study," I pleaded.

"I'm not smart like you, okay?"

She phrased it like a compliment but said it like an insult.

"Meaning?"

"*Meaning*, I took eighth-grade math in eighth grade, not fourth. If I don't study, I fail. You're the only person I know who gets to have both."

"Both?"

"The *day* and the *A*," she said. "Most of us have to choose one or the other." Then with a kind smile she added, "If I didn't like you so much I'd have a real problem with that."

I could have made a case for half-a-day and a B+, but she was over it. So I asked what she wanted to study first.

"Thank you." Vanessa grinned. "I owe you."

"Yeah, that worked real well for us last time," I teased, referring to the night she was supposed to change my grades but ditched me instead.

She rolled her eyes playfully. "I owe you twice, then."

After that it was all business.

Now it's 12:30 AM and Vanessa just farted in her sleep. I got my giggle.

Lily Bader-Huffman

Jagger

Nov. 14.

The freshman play is on Saturday.

Wicked.

Audri will be rehearsing all week.

She said I probably won't see her until after the show.

LIE #62: That sucks.

I wouldn't be able to see her much this week anyway and now I don't have to lie.

Lie about why I need to be present. Focused. Engaged.

Why I need to attend one, if not two, Mini Mavericks meetings.

Why I need to quit taking off at all hours of the night to do lord knows what.

Why I can, and WILL, kick my drug habit.
I did more than enough lying to Dr. Lloyd.

Q: Daniel, what is your drug of choice?
A: (LIE #63) Tobacco.

Q: *Tobacco?*
A: Ugh. It sounds so ugly when you say it.

Q: Sorry. Just to be clear we're talking about cigarettes.
A: Yes.

Q: Only cigarettes.
A: Yes.

Q: The kind that are legal?
A: Yes, if you're over 18. I'm not.

Q: Have you noticed a shift in your behavior since you started taking, er, cigarettes?
A: (LIES #64–74) Big-time. I've been restless, agitated, jittery. I'm always thinking about my next smoke. Or where I can get the money to buy them. I've got every cashier in every store dialed. I know who will card me and who won't. Then there's that smell. I have to hide it from my teachers, friends, family . . . It's exhausting. I'm so ashamed.

Q: Does that mean you're ready to quit?

A: Yes.

LIE #75: I think my behavior has been a cry for help.

... And on it went.

After the evaluation Dr. Lloyd told Mother and Father that a treatment facility would not be necessary. He recommended chewing gum, physical activity, and deep breathing.

I saw him today for a follow-up and urine test.

He's pleased to report I am doing great. Not a single trace of nicotine.

Father bought me an alligator briefcase to congratulate me.

He has the same one. He uses his for work and suggests I use mine for my Mini Mavericks meetings. But I should feel free to use it at school too.

— No way, I told him.

— Why?

LIE #76: I'd hate for something to happen to it.

The truth is, it reminds me that I'm a liar. Not only to Audri, but Mother and Father too. And that lying to family, especially when they have always been honest with you, wears on a guy's conscience after a while.

They don't deserve it.

Fine, maybe they deserve it a little bit because they gave me this name.

Had they just taken an extra minute to think things through they might have realized that mass producing T-words and naming me Daniel Ponnowitz could lead to DanPonn down the road.

But they didn't. So here we are.

Sheridan

11.14.12

INT. SHERIDAN's BEDROOM—DESK—NIGHT.

Channeling CHRISTINA AGUILERA in her latest video, "Your Body," SHERIDAN wraps a blue bandanna around her head and fastens it with one of her brothers' clip-on ties. The bow is centered perfectly between her eyebrows. Tousled blond hair spills over her shoulders. Her lipstick is pale pink. She is at one with the paused image on her computer screen. She is fierce.

Christina. I, like you, am ready to own my curves. To celebrate my cravings and indulge my needs—none of which involve putting down this Charleston Chew and hitting the treadmill.

You see, I've spent four days trying to whittle my middle and reduce my caboose, but all I'm losing is steam. *Wicked* is Saturday and between rehearsals and homework, I don't have the strength.

One could argue that I'm an understudy, making jumping jacks in the wings while Octavia is onstage making a mockery of the craft—a viable option. But I am a professional. I have made a commitment to the theater and I will see it through to the best of my ability. If the elastic band on my underwear digs into my lower abdomen as a result, so be it. That's not to say I won't slim down for my TV series. I will, starting Monday.

I just watched "Your Body" again. That Christina is one powerful pear.

To Be Continued . . .

END SCENE.

Vanessa

November 16th

I stayed at Lily's for the past two nights. All I did was study. The only break I took was to sleep, eat, and hydrate. It was awesome. Ver? Now it's Lily I'm worried about.

Mandy stopped by yesterday to say that *Seventeen* magazine and *Good Morning America* want to interview them about *Horace Power*. It's *that* viral.

Lily was so excited she couldn't study anymore. She thinks grades aren't the be-all and end-all. She's wearing that stupid shirt.

I know she's unequivocally brilliant, but what if she seizes so much of the day her GPA drops? What if she gets pulled from Noble again? I don't want her to go.

The bell just rang. Wish me luck—I need to kick some major A's.[101]

> *You must find the place inside of you where nothing is impossible.*

—Deepak Chopra

---

[101] Ha!

DUFFY

Friday

Feeling = When a guy gets slam-dumped twice in one week, a gym full of Screamers doesn't hurt.

Feeling = It helps. A lot.

Feeling = It's also good for business.

After we slayed the Dragons 44–20 on their own soil, all these girls started saying how hot I was or looked or smelled. I must have sent twenty dudes to the Trendemic site.

The whole ride back to Noble, the team is busting on me because I didn't get a single number.

Feeling = I'm not gonna text some random chick from Woodland because she says, A phone isn't the only thing your jeans are charging.

Then I remember that's what a decent guy would say, and I need to be respected. So I say, I have plenty of numbers already. I can't handle any more.

They ask me to share some with them. I say get your own. They say they try, but it doesn't work. I promise to show them how it's done after our next game.

Feeling = I wish I knew.

— LATER

Sheridan

11.17.12

INT. NOBLE HIGH—STARLIGHT AUDITORIUM DRESSING ROOM C—30 MINUTES UNTIL CURTAIN.

SHERIDAN turns off CHRISTINA AGUILERA, removes her headphones, and sighs. Her green-faced REFLEC-TION sighs back.

Will you please move over? (A Munchkin, not the edible kind.) *The mirror is for the actors who will actually be onstage.*

Try not to fall off. It's a far drop for a little guy like you. (Me, wanting to hang him by that stupid red curlicue on top of his head.)

Witch.

Extra.

Understudy.

Under . . . everything!

With that, I went next door to wish Audri broken legs. Because that's what superlatively good sports do.

Her dressing room was crackling with nervous energy. Foreheads in hands, nail-biting, pacing. Something more than backstage jitters was at play here. I could see it in the armpits of Mr. Kimball's shirt. They don't usually yellow until the middle of act two.

I was about to ask Audri what was going on. Then I got Octavia's text:

GOOD LUCK.

The words leapt off the screen like flying monkeys.

She's not coming? (Me.)

Last-minute tickets to Justin Timberlake. (Audri.)

How can she skip out on her role, her cast, her crew, her audience . . . for a concert? She's worse than . . . What's the animal that eats its young?

Hamster? (Audri.)

Not as cute.

Charlie Sheen? (Mr. Fluvinack, the piano player.)

Wolf spider? (Audri.)

Yes. Octavia is a wolf spider. Sorry. I know you guys are tight but—

We were. Not anymore. Not after this. (Audri.)

I hadn't given much thought to what any of this meant for

me until Mr. Kimball handed me a black dress and wig and said, *It's show time*.

Those two words canceled out Octavia's two words. When I stepped onto the stage ten minutes later, only three thoughts entered my mind.

1. I finally get to play opposite Audri.
2. I need one more coat of green makeup.
3. Cheeses, this dress is tight.

CUT TO:

INT. STARLIGHT AUDITORIUM—CURTAIN CALL—BEST NIGHT EVER.

SHERIDAN and AUDRI exchange luminous smiles as they join hands and walk to the foot of the stage. The APPLAUSE is thunderous. The two LEADS bow and then blow kisses to the CAST behind them. Then the ORCHESTRA. Then the sobbing, yellow-pitted MR. KIMBALL. When SHERIDAN and AUDRI bow again, the AUDIENCE stands.

I'm not kidding. It was superlative on every level. Audri and I had tears in our eyes, it was that magical. Not just the standing O, but the fact that we did it together. The way it was always supposed to be.

The house lights came on and Mr. Kimball asked everyone to take their seats because there was something he wanted to say. Audri and I turned to go back into the cast line, but Mr.

Kimball reached for my arm and pulled me back. What he wanted to say was about me.

Sheridan Spencer is a true professional. More so than anyone I have ever worked with, be it on Broadway, off, or off-off. She was always on time, always paying attention, and ready to step in at a moment's notice. She proved that tonight when she was literally given ONE. MOMENT'S. NOTICE.

MORE APPLAUSE.

MR. KIMBALL turns to SHERIDAN and speaks directly to her.

My only regret is not casting you as the lead from the very beginning. One thing's for sure. I will never make that mistake again.

MORE APPLAUSE.

I didn't care about his pits. I hugged that man hard.

Sheridan Spencer, will you please take one last bow!

SHERIDAN bows. As she straightens back up she hears *zzzzzrrrpppppp*. A chilly breeze licks the left side of her torso.

What the—

Your costume! (Mr. Kimball.)

THE CURSE!

SHERIDAN pinches the seams, forcing them to meet, but they refuse. A ten-pack of ChipClips and a glue gun can't save her now. Her chickens-with-glasses underwear, the rolls of flesh; all of it exposed.

Suddenly, the AUDIENCE seems different—childish

317

and unkind. Like the comedy-tragedy masks of ancient Greece, some laugh, some weep, all in slow motion. SHERIDAN gazes into the white lights, wondering if she is dying. She prays that angels will guide her safely to the wings. But it's too late. The cell phones have arrived. And they're hungry. Hungry for a sound bite or a 140-character snack to post at the all-you-can-tweet buffet.

SHERIDAN opens her mouth to speak. CHRISTINA AGUILERA comes out.

You are in the presence of a fat girl. Not big-boned. Not jolly. Not bloated. FAT. And guess what? I'm happy. I'd rather be celebrated for my body of work than my body of abs and I got a standing ovation tonight. So I'm not going to run away and hide because I split my costume. I'm going to grin and pear it. Because I am a professional and that's what we do.

To Be Continued...

END SCENE.

DUFFY

Sunday

I owed $533.85 to Trendemic before we played the Dragons on Friday.

After we played I earned $589.00

Now I have a $55.15 credit.

Balance Due: $0

ZERO!

Zeeeeeeeeeeeeeeeeeeeeeeeeeeeeeeeeeeeeeeeeeeeeeeeeeeeeeeeeeeeero.

I am Jay-Zero!

Meet my wife Beyonc-paid!

And our lovely daughter Blue Ivy.

Why Blue? Because I'm not in the red.
Why Ivy? Because Ivy paid Anton back!

Feeling = I am freeeeeeeeeeeeeeeeeeeeeeeeeeeeee.

Free to smell like skin again. Free to wear jeans that don't need to be charged overnight. Free to dialogue with the Screamers and ignore the dudes. Free to hang with my buddies and show them how a real man plays pickup.

Feeling = Respected.

— LATER

Lily

Tuesday, November 20, 2012

Mrs. Martin called her AP students in for one-on-ones to go over our test results before her maternity leave. My B+ average surprised her, but not as much as my reaction.

"That's a *bummer*?" she said. "That's it?"

I nodded.

She sighed. "Lily, I really expected great things from you. Now it seems like you're just giving up. Is something going on at home?"

"No. I just can't handle the pressure. I think I should switch back to the normal program."

Was I proud to be messing with a woman who was trying to

help me *whilst* growing a human inside her body? A body that looked like it had been attached to a fire hydrant and filled to capacity? So much so that every time she tried to cross her legs I heard sloshing water? No. I was not proud at all, but I had to consider the alternative.

A straight-A student—all AP classes—could not go on national television and tout a movement that encourages students to "Seize the day, not the A." It's disingenuous.

When I told Vanessa about my meeting she was more shocked than Mrs. Martin.

"You *asked* to be moved?" she said, slamming her locker.

"I'm tired."

"Oh please," Vanessa said, scratching her arm. "It's Mandy and that whole *Horace Power*, isn't it?"

"No! I choked," I said. I spotted Blake and waved him over so we could grab lunch. "Food truck today?"

"Lily!" Vanessa snapped. "What's wrong with you? It's like you don't even care."

"Don't worry, I won't get kicked out again," I said. "My parents let me do what I want now. I'm allowed to be normal!"

"Ugh!" Vanessa shuddered. "Don't say that word."

Blake appeared, wallet in hand. "What word?"

"I'm not allowed to say it."

Vanessa rolled her eyes. *"Normal."*

"What's wrong with nor—"

"Don't say it!" I snapped.

Blake covered his mouth.

"Mrs. Martin is making me switch back to the N program." Vanessa sniffled. "Now I'll never be a Phoenix Five. I'll never be the best. I'll never be—"

"Overscheduled?" I tried.

"I like being overscheduled," Vanessa said. "It's being N that stresses me out."

I put my arm around her, wishing we could switch identities like they do in the movies. She could be the exception and I could be typical.

"At least we'll be together," I tried.

During lunch we talked about our plans for Thanksgiving, the grossness of raisins in stuffing, and ways to mess with Mike's customers on Black Friday.

Vanessa participated, but her mind was elsewhere. Someplace dark and distant. A secret mental lair, where her grandest plans are hatched and her shameless thoughts are hidden. The place she goes to figure out that next big move. I know because I have one too.

I went to that dark and distant place before I wrote my exams last Friday. It's where I decided to botch my answers so I could get released from the AP program. It's where I will celebrate all the seizing I do from this day forward.

Lily Bader-Huffman

324

Vanessa

November 21st

Wonder Bread Words[102] are everyday words that offer zero value. Never attempt to use these words in conversation or writing. They are useless.

I'm *good*, how are you?
What a *pleasant* day.
That book was *interesting*.
Divorce is *common*.

....

[102] Note: Ms. Silver, I made this term up; therefore, I am not citing it.

Now, watch what happens when I replace these Wonder Bread Words with spicier terms.

I'm *invincible*, how are you?
What an *SPF15* kind of day.
That book was a *nail-biter*.
Divorce is *quitting*.

See the difference?

Wonder Bread Words tamp out the flavor and make that which they are describing bland. This is why I itch when a Wonder Bread Word is used to describe me, my academic career, my world in any way. I must have flavor.

Ver? I know Lily wants flavor too. Everyone does. My guess is that she's afraid of trying and failing again. I was about to test this theory on her during lunch, but Blake joined us and we moved on. In hindsight I'm glad we did.

This way Lily will be totally surprised when I tell her what I did. I know. I know. I know. It's wrong. It's illegal on every level. But it's foolproof. Mrs. Martin will be gone for the rest of the school year and she doesn't even have a replacement yet. Besides, it's not like I took us from F's to A's. More like B's to A's for me and B+'s to A's for Lily. I owed her two, and this will feel more like three.

Happy Thanksgiving, Lil!

Jagger

Nov. 21.

I get a call from Randy's Exotic Pets during second period.

I figure I'm getting busted for saying I live there so I shoot the call to voice mail.

Turns out my sugar glider is in.

They want me to pick it up before Thanksgiving. It needs love and won't survive the long weekend in a cage.

I skip Chemistry and bike over.

Randy is there when I pull up. It's the first time I've ever seen the guy.

I pictured a hairy Harley-riding kind of guy with a denim vest and eyes so squinty you wonder how he sees.

Wrong.

Real Randy is skinny and hairless as a stick bug. His mouth is wide and he doesn't blink his bulgy brown eyes the whole time I'm there.

Me? I blink like crazy when he says all these high schoolers have been dropping cans of food at his door for Thanksgiving.

LIE #77: I wonder why?

He says his store got flooded during the hurricane and everyone is pitching in. That's the kind of community we live in. We're lucky.

— I agree, I say.

LIE #77.5: I don't agree. Not completely, anyway. I do agree that we're lucky to live here. Any community that's not whipping T-words at me makes me feel lucky. But the food he got was meant for me. People at school have been donating it because they think I'll be alone with the pets over the holiday.

Randy steps into the back and comes out with a palm-sized rodent.

It has Randy's eyes, a pink nose, and a skunk stripe down its back.

I try not to make those sounds girls make when they see babies and kittens, but the thing is pretty cute so I go, *heh*.

— Got a cage for it? I ask.

She's a marsupial, Randy says. She'd rather be in your pocket.

LIE #78: Cool.

But it's not cool because I rode my bike and I don't want to squish her.

— That'll be two hundred and fifty dollars, Randy tells me.

I give him my Visa and then ask for a bag.

Randy laughs a booger right out of his nose. It lands on his sleeve. We both pretend it didn't.

— You can't put her in a bag. We do sell bonding pouches and sleeping sacks if you're interested.

— I am.

I bike off like Elliott with E.T.

Last thing I need is to be spotted talking to a mouse in a glitter purse so I go straight to Audri's.

I call her and tell her to meet me at her house.

She doesn't even have to think about it. She doesn't care if she misses class. She just says yes because she trusts me.

I'm sitting on the steps when she gets there.

Sugar is inside the purse, which is inside my shirt.

I'm wearing it like a necklace so the pouch is against my belly button.

Every time Sugar squirms it tickles.

Audri asks why I'm giggling. I say because I'm happy to see her. Most of that is true so I'm not counting it as a lie.

She unlocks the door. I follow her inside, taking long sniffs of her vanilla perfume. It's been a while since I smelled it.

Too long.

Ignore the mail, she says.

Mom has been working so much lately. I swear we're going to get our power shut off if she doesn't start paying those bills.

Girls love explaining their messes. So I look at the pile like it matters.

Then I see it. An envelope addressed to her mother. The return address says Legacy, but the street address is mine.

Audri's mom got the Ponnowitz family holiday card!

LIE #79: Is it thirsty in here?

Audri giggles and leaves to grab us some waters.

I take the card and stuff it down the back of my jeans.

I wanted to make a big deal out of Sugar, but now my heart is pumping fight-or-flight feelings through my entire body and I can't think straight.

So I pull out the pouch when Audri gets back and say, here.

Audri tries to look excited about a pink felt glitter purse.

Open it, I say.

She does.

Then makes those girly sounds.

She doesn't know who to hug first. Me or Sugar.

She chooses Sugar.

I'm glad.

My heart was thrashing. I didn't want her to feel it.

Audri puts her hand in the pouch.

Sugar flies out.

A hairy square with dangling feet.

We chase her all over the living room.

It's hilarious because we can tell she wants to play.

She flies around the couch, through the kitchen, and into the pantry.

We follow her inside and shut the door to trap her.

She lands on Audri's shoulder.

We're panting and laughing and making girly sounds.

Then the front door clicks open.

Audri freezes, then mouths, *Mom*. She slides a finger across her throat to let me know she's dead if she gets caught skipping school.

We don't move.

I wish my heart would slow down so I can hear what's going on.

Then it does.

And I hear.

There's a man with her.

They're fumbling. Kissing. Mumbling.

Audri's eyes fill with tears and I know it's the man who has been dating her mother.

The man who broke up her parents' marriage.

She whispers, Wreck-It Ralph.

She wants to open the door and bust them.

She wants to know who he is.

She needs to know.

I stop her.

I say she doesn't want to know. Not like this.

Maybe it's my dad, she tries. What if they're getting back together?

It's not.

How do you know?

LIE #80: I don't.

– Let's peek.

– Audri, no.

– I need to see him.

– Audri!

She pushes me away from the door and cracks it open.

Sugar nestles into Audri's hair.

We peer out.

The man is in a navy-blue business suit. He is tall and fit. Neatly combed dark hair. His alligator briefcase rests on the back of the couch.

– See, I say, tucking us back inside the pantry. It's not your dad.

A giant claw grips the inside of my stomach and twists.

Tears spill out the bottoms of her glasses.

I ask if she's ever seen that man before.

– No, she says. Have you?

LIE #81: No.

I have.

His name is Richard Ponnowitz IV.

He is the CEO of Legacy Hygienics. The family values company.

He is my father.

333

EPILOGUE

Hello, Partner,

I trust you'll find this a more satisfying place to stop than last time? Less abrupt? More closure? I hope so.

Duffy is all paid off and on his way to becoming a celebrated ladies' man. Sheridan is on the fast track to stardom. Lily is the soon-to-be-leader of the Pub world. Vanessa has an unobstructed view of the top. And Jagger is about to score some major bargaining power with Pops.

It's comforting to see our future Phoenix Fivers on the rise, isn't it? That's because you know we're not bad people. We're good people who made bad choices. Not because our lives depended on it, but because our dreams did. And young people are supposed to follow their dreams. We're encouraged to pursue them at any cost. So we follow and pursue without stopping to check the price. Because sacrifice is the ugly side of success and who wants to see that?

I wish I had....

Until Next Time,

Credits

Story Editor
Erin Stein

Production Editor
Barbara Bakowski

Copy Editor
Ashley Mason

Design
**Liz Casal, Sasha Illingworth,
and David Caplan**

Marketing
**Andrew Smith, Ann Dye,
and Jennifer LaBracio**

PR
Melanie Chang and Kristina Aven

Lisi's Genius Editorial Assistant
Alisha Maddocks

Lisi's Genius Office Elf
Yep, Alisha again

Free but Invaluable Support
**Kevin, Luke, Jess-Jess,
Beebs, Pepper, Gottliebs,
Harrisons, Coopers**

Fierce Agent
Richard Abate

Fierce Agent's Fierce Assistant
Melissa Kahn

Fancy LA Attorney
Alex Kohner

Fancy LA Associate
Logan Clare

Daily Latte and Laughter
Everyone at Laguna Coffee Company

Loyal Friends
**Anyone over thirty years old
who I don't pay, is not related
to me, and is reading this**

Loyal Readers
You—always, always you

Special thanks to
Sheridan Spencer
for inspiring me to write my
acknowledgments like a credit roll.
So fun!